MYSTERY MEN
(& WOMEN)

Volume Two

Airship 27 Productions

AN AIRSHIP 27 PRODUCTION

Mystery Men (& Women)
Volume Two

Updated collection ©2022 Airship 27 Productions

"The Red Badge Attacks" © 2011 Mark Halegua and Andrew Salmon
"Lair of the Mole People" © 2011 By Gregory Bastianelli
"Dock Doyle" © 2011 Adam Lance Garcia
"Just Another Day at the Office" © 2011 Derrick Ferguson

An Airship 27 Production
www.airship27.com

Editor: Ron Fortier
Associate Editor: Charles Saunders
Production Designer: Rob Davis.

ISBN: 978-1-953589-22-4

Printed in the United States of America

10 9 8 7 6 5 4 3 2 1

MYSTERY MEN (& Women) Volume 2

-Table of Contents-

The RED BADGE
"The Red Badge Attacks"

By Mark Halegua & Andrew Salmon

The office of Bruno Carbone had been designed to represent a respectable place of business in which an honest businessman could conduct his affairs. However the office was no more respectable than the man himself who ran a criminal empire from within its tawdry walls. Overstuffed, mismatched furnishings and shadowed corners a little too black characterized the place. The low ceiling gave one the impression they were stepping into a tomb. For many of the visitors to this den of evil, that impression had proved accurate.

"What! The warehouse burned down?" Carbone roared at the two men seated opposite him. He shot to his feet, placed his square fists on the rough desktop, and stood glaring down at the men. "This your idea of a gag?"

"No, Boss!" One of the men, Moe was his name, squirmed in his seat. His hands clutched feverishly at the beat up fedora in his lap and he started to sweat in his black leather jacket. "We was leaving the warehouse, me and Curly (he indicated the man seated next to him) and Max and Duey. We'd just put away the booze and horse, when this strange sound came out of nowhere. Like a rat squealing or something, right, Curly?"

"Yeah Boss," Curly nodded eagerly, the collar of his dark turtleneck sweater suddenly choking him. "Like Moe says, except it sounded more like a giant rat, you know."

Moe took up the thread of the tale. "Well, next thing you know, Max and Duey are down. And this voice tells us to tell you, uh ..."

Carbone was a dark complexioned man with hair as black as coal. As he listened, his face darkened further, with rage. He was of medium height but heavily built, muscles testing the limits of his expensive suit. A cigar was pincered between two thick fingers of one hand resting on the desk, ash spilled unnoticed on the polished wood. He raised that fist and jabbed the cigar at the mobsters, "Come on, spill!"

Moe dropped his hat while he fumbled to unzip his jacket. Sweat trickled down his forehead. "Well, that is, uh, he told us to tell you to get out of town. Shut down the operation and get out. Says it's his city, now."

"He said what!" The cigar twisted like a pretzel in Carbone's hand. "Nobody tells Bruno Carbone what to do! Batelli!"

From one stygian corner behind Carbone's desk, a tall, thin man stepped into view. His skin was so white he resembled an albino at first glance. However further inspection revealed a pair of dark, forbidding, merciless eyes. The man named Batelli smiled cruelly as he withdrew his right hand from behind his back. That hand held a scarred, pitted baseball bat which dangled along one leg of his ill-fitting suit. "Bat" Batelli was known for his skill with a bat and it was a reputation not earned on a baseball diamond. The enjoyment he got from applying this skill was also well documented and feared by the underworld.

"No, no, Boss, please," Moe begged. "I didn't say it, the guy who eighty-sixed Max and Duey told me to tell you. And then he threw this on the ground when I asked who he was." Moe pawed at one jacket pocket, then yanked a dark red badge out and held it up.

Carbone made a short slashing gesture behind him. "Hold on, Batelli." The crime boss thrust his hand out to Moe. "Give me that!"

Carbone examined the badge, turning it this way and that in his hands. "Looks like a police badge, except for the color and there ain't no number on it. It doesn't say Central City. Or any other city either. What's it supposed to mean?"

Moe, slightly relieved his boss's attention was focused elsewhere, replied eagerly. "I don't know Boss, honest. It lands on the ground, I pick it up and he tells us to git out quick, which we did. We knew not to come here direct like, in case he was following, so we took the long way, making sure we weren't tailed."

Carbone nodded curtly "That may be the smartest thing you've done your whole stinking life. This was what, a couple hours ago?"

"Yes, Boss," Curly replied.

Carbone stabbed down on the intercom. "Get in here."

The door opened and two men entered. Both were slim types with slimy grins twisting their blunt features. "Alright, Nunzio, get out there and find out who this Red Badge is," Carbone addressed the man on the left. "He's a rat who needs squashing before I lose any more money." He turned his attention to the second man. "Alberti, we need another place to store stuff, another warehouse. Find me something. And a new office. There's no telling if these two mooks have the brains to shake a tail."

The two men nodded and exited.

Carbone returned to studying the badge. Suddenly faint tendrils of smoke came off its crimson surface. Seconds later, Carbone dropped it like a red hot coal as he jerked his hand back. Everyone in the room watched the badge melt into a shapeless red lump. The desk under the badge started to smolder and char.

"That damn thing burnt me!" Carbone turned to the two goons. "All right you two. I've heard enough of your excuses. Batelli." Carbone nodded at the seated mobsters. "Make an example out of these two. Slow, painful and permanent. Wait, keep one of 'em around. He'll need to be able to talk about it. Eventually."

"Bat" Batelli's shark's grin widened and the still night was shattered by the sounds of crunching bones and pounded flesh. These sounds were finally drowned out by the screams.

•••

The tallest of the stabbing cluster of skyscrapers that made up the downtown core of Central City was Cade Plaza. The building was made even more impressive by the soaring transmission tower on top. That tower broadcast the city's most popular radio station to waiting listeners.

Into this impressive edifice strode the trim figure of Al Spade. He was of above average height with thick, wavy brown hair and piercing blue eyes. He stepped lightly into an elevator, greeted the car operator who took him up to the 20th floor, the home of KACM.

Spade stepped from the elevator and collided with Tommy Balboa, a page at the station.

"Hey, there, kid," Spade said, amicably. "How's tricks? How's that mom of yours?"

Tommy's wide brown eyes grew even wider in his lean face when he saw who he had crashed into. "Hello, Mr. Spade! I'm okay, I guess." He swept an unruly lock of black hair off his forehead. "So's my Ma. She says to tell you thanks for getting her that secretary job! She says Mr. Mays is great to work for."

"My pleasure."

"I want to thank you, too, for getting me this job here at the station. Things sure have been tough for Ma and me since Pa got killed."

Spade smiled warmly down at the teenager. "Think nothing of it, kid. Glad to help."

"Well, Mr. Spade, if you ever need anything, just ask. Ma says she'll send you some of her lasagna."

"I'll keep your offer in mind, Tommy. As for your mom's lasagna, that's one I'll take you up on right now!"

Spade bade the youth farewell and moved purposefully over to the receptionist's desk where Ms. Maybell Haskell, a pretty, dark-haired young woman sat primly.

"Any messages for me, Maybell?"

"Mr. Mays called but he didn't leave a message."

"Thank you, Maybell."

Maybell's enchanting brown eyes flashed. "My pleasure, Mr. Spade."

Spade turned towards the offices beyond the reception area and did not see the adoring, amorous look Maybell cast after him.

Before Spade could reach his cluttered desk, Herman Ross, the station manager, stepped out of his office and approached. "Al, you're on in ten. What do you have for me today?"

"Plenty. And, Herm, most of it's tied to Carbone's outfit."

The two men walked past the desks to the broadcast booths. "Great if you can make it stick," Ross said. "What else?"

"A drive by tragedy on Broadway with assurances from Captain Kuark that Central's finest will get their man. My sources tell me O'Leary's bunch was hitting one of Fleisch's joints and the innocents got in the way."

Ross snorted derisively as they stopped at one of the booths. "Word is Kuark's in Fleisch's pocket."

Spade placed his hand on the doorknob. "You're not buying that line that Kuark is just out of his depth as Captain? Some say he was a good officer once."

"We were all something once," Ross said, morosely. Then as he walked away, he added over his shoulder, "Get on the air. Blast those guys!"

Spade was just settling into his seat when the booth door burst open and Tommy rushed in. He thrust a teletype page at Spade.

"What is it?" Spade asked.

"Mr. Spade! An hour ago two of Carbone's gang were found in an alley not far from the warehouse at Grey Hook. One was dead, the other beat up pretty bad. He's at Saints and the docs are working on him. Looks like someone went over them with a pipe or something."

Spade took the copy from the boy. "Thanks, kid. Now scoot. I'm on."

The intro music flared up in the booth just as Tommy closed the door. This was followed by the announcer's voice over the squawk box:

"It's 4 o'clock on KACM, your anti-crime radio station. Time for Al Spade and 'Calling a Spade a Spade'. Take it away, Al!"

Al gripped the microphone in one fist and leaned forward. "Hello citizens of Central City. Last night a terrific explosion blew up Boss Carbone's Grey Hook warehouse, taking that mob's booze, drugs, stolen cars and property with it. Who was behind it? No one knows for sure. Police found two of Carbone's thugs dead outside the flaming wreck."

Spade took a sip of water. "In other news: a drive by shooting on Broadway an hour ago killed three people, one of them an infant girl, and wounded four others. The shooters had targeted one of Boss Fleisch's gambling and numbers den. Captain Kuark of the CCPD says he'll get the shooters soon."

Spade's grip tightened on the microphone and he grimaced before continuing. "Now let's call a spade a spade. Captain Kuark is as incompetent a police captain as this city has ever seen. He's held the reins for over a year and crime rates have risen across the board. The man hasn't even been able to clean out the corruption in his own department. When is the Mayor going to remove him and appoint someone who can protect the citizens of this city? Election day draws near, and let's call a spade a spade, if something isn't done quickly, Mayor Carlton, you won't be Mayor much longer."

Spade picked up the teletype Tommy had left. "Another interesting tidbit just in. Two of Carbone's mob were found not far from their boss's destroyed warehouse. Their injuries suggest they were beaten with a blunt object. Looks like the work of Carbone's enforcer, 'Bat' Batelli. Well, at least the garbage is getting hauled regular. This is Al Spade, calling a spade a spade. Now a word from our sponsors."

•••

The street on the West Side appeared deserted in the 1A.M. stillness. However the speakeasy at the end of the block was well known and the walls vibrated with loud conversation, the clink of glasses and the click of pool balls sent hissing along velvet. The patrons, lost in their illicit revelry, caroused in ignorance of what was about to transpire.

A man in a dark crimson duster with a flat-topped, wide-brimmed hat of similar hue suddenly launched through the entrance, and drove two pile-driver punches into the bouncer at the door. The first doubled the man over, the second smashed down on the back of the bouncer's head. The man crumpled and lay at the scarlet assailant's feet.

The man in red growled. "Everyone out! Now!"

The order spurred a mug seated at a back table to get up and paw inside his coat for a pistol. Before he could pull the weapon, a crimson streak flashed across the distance and impaled the man's gun hand. The man stared stupidly down at the crimson knife handle sticking out of his palm, then let out a roar before overturning a table as he tumbled.

The man in red spoke again. "I said everyone out! This place is going down!"

This time his command had the desired effect. Women and men scampered for the door. The man in red stepped away from the exit and moved quickly past the fleeing patrons toward the back of the room. There he pressed a partially concealed button near a rack of pool cues. A portion of the wall slid away. A goon standing on the inside of that wall gaped in surprise and received a stout jab to the face before tumbling to the floor, senseless. The man in red stepped over the sprawled form and through the entryway to stand facing men in tuxedos and women in evening gowns huddled around various gambling tables.

"Anyone in here five minutes from now will die!"

The croupier from the nearest craps table barreled towards the crimson figure, swinging his stick. For this action he received a scarlet boot buried in his guts. As the man in red stepped over the fallen croupier, he stamped down on the stick hand, bones snapping.

A huge gunsel stepped forward, aiming a revolver. Before he could pull the trigger, the man in red had drawn a duo of odd-shaped pistols from beneath the scarlet folds of his coat. Crimson fingers squeezed the triggers and the guns made a peculiar noise like rat claws across a chalkboard. The huge man staggered as he was hit in the elbow of his gun arm and the right knee. He dropped his gun and collapsed to the floor, writhing in pain.

The rest of the room's occupants had seen enough. Men and women streamed from the room while the bartender pulled out a shotgun. The man in red whirled to face him and his guns made that low, grating noise again. The first shot tore through the bartender's throat, the second burrowed into the man's forehead.

Glancing about the almost deserted room, the man in red spied the two crippled crooks as they crawled away, dragging the doorman with them. No one else remained. From the folds of his coat, the crimson attacker withdrew several black spheres. He turned stubby handles jutting from the orbs, arming them, and placed the grenades on the tabletops. This done, he calmly exited.

The patrons who had not yet fled milled about outside the place and several tried to get a look at the scarlet avenger but the man's features were concealed beneath his hat brim.

The man in red walked to a crimson motorcycle, straddled it and appeared to start the motor, however no roar accompanied the action. Soundlessly, the cycle rolled forward, exhaust plumes shooting out the rear. The bike passed close to one of the crippled men. The man in red tossed a red badge which landed near the man's outstretched hand. A moment later several explosions from within the building erupted and the structure collapsed. By the time the spectators had pawed the smoke and dust out of their eyes, the man in red was gone.

•••

At noon the next day the door of the AA Fix-It Shop opened and Aaron Agnew, Proprietor, stepped out onto bustling Commercial Street. Agnew was in his early sixties, bald, wearing wire-rim glasses and a white smock. Stomach rumbling and thoughts of a sandwich and coffee at the corner diner on his mind, he locked the door and turned to find two men standing close behind him. One wore a suit and had a fedora pulled low on his forehead. The other was clad in a gray turtleneck sweater and dark cloth cap.

The man with the fedora stared down at Agnew, asking, "You own this place?"

"As a matter of fact I do," Agnew replied, a puzzled look on his face. "I am closing for lunch just now. If you'll come back in an hour, I'll be happy to help you."

The shop owner stepped to one side to walk around the two men but the man with the cloth cap placed a restraining hand on his arm.

"Our business won't wait, Pops. You need to hear us out."

Agnew looked over the two men, both at least a head taller than he and brawnier.

"I think I understand," he said, then reluctantly unlocked the door and ushered the men in. The man in the cloth cap paused at the door, locked it, and lowered the shade. The man with the fedora strode to the shop counter and leaned on it, insolently.

Agnew stepped behind the counter of his cluttered shop, straightened his smock and regarded the men frankly. "How may I help you gentlemen?"

"Actually we're here to help you, Mr. Agnew." The man with the fedora explained. "We've noticed this repair shop does good business and want to offer you insurance. Against damage to the property and the items you repair.

"Really?" Agnew deadpanned. "I already have fire insurance and there isn't much here worth stealing so I don't think I'll need your insurance."

"Don't be too hasty. What we offer is special coverage. For example, supposing someone came into the shop and, I don't know, started tossing things on the floor, smashing countertops. Things like that. You'd be insured against that, you see. Call it breakage insurance."

The man in the cloth cap flicked a table top radio off the counter and it smashed on the floor.

"Hey, I just fixed that!"Agnew complained.

"That's exactly the type of thing I'm talking about." The man with the fedora gestured to his associate to hold off. "See here, Agnew. This is a small place and we're not unreasonable. $25 a week sounds about right for the kind of breakage insurance we can provide."

No longer attempting civility, Agnew glared at the two thugs. "Well, I don't have

"Don't be too hasty. What we offer is special coverage. Call it breakage insurance."

that kind of money today. Can you come back tomorrow, say around 6:00 PM?"

The man with the fedora smiled a crocodile smile. "See, that's all there is to it. Tomorrow at six, it is. Enjoy your lunch."

•••

Across town at Cade Plaza, Al Spade was finishing up the day's radio broadcast.

"Last night some of our better citizens, swells all, were rudely interrupted while putting down some bets in one of Boss Carbone's gambling establishments on the West side. According to some wild reports, a man in dark red western gear burst in and took down some of the toughest mugs in Carbone's gang, then blew the place. One witness claims the man tossed a red police badge at one of the goons."

Al gave his listeners a chance to absorb this before continuing.

"A red police badge?" he went on. "Is this Red Badge character a member of Central City's finest? I asked the Mayor and got a curt 'no comment' for my effort. So I took the matter to Captain Kuark. His response was more expressive. I quote: 'Absolutely not. And he's not doing the citizens of this city any good blowing up buildings or masquerading as a police officer. People could have been hurt or worse. I'm asking this man, this criminal, to turn himself in before he does any more damage.' Kuark may not know how to keep the streets clean but the man doesn't mince words. As for the masquerading as a police officer remark, I wonder at the good Captain's ire. Kuark's been masquerading as a police officer for years.

"Well listeners, calling a spade a spade, I think this guy, this Red Badge, may be a big help for us. Cop or not, he's doing a better job on crime than our police force. Until next time, this is Al Spade, signing off."

Tommy caught up with Spade in the radio personality's office.

"Hi, Mr. Spade," Tommy began, then fell mute when he saw the man doing something strange with a pencil and paper. "What you doing there?"

Spade looked up from his work. "Hello, kid. I guess you could call it investigative reporting."

"It looks like you're rubbing that pencil sideways over that wrinkled paper. What does that do? How is that investigative reporting?"

Spade set the paper aside and leaned back in his chair. "Well, kid, when people write things down on pads they press down hard on the top sheet and the pages underneath take an impression. Then they tear off the top sheet and take it with them. The next page of the pad looks blank, but, if you run the side of a pencil across the page, the surface turns black from the carbon and impressions from the page above will be visible. Because the writing on the sheet is slightly lower than the rest of the page, the letters show up white and you can read what was written on the sheet they tore off."

"That's a neat trick! Where'd you get that paper?"

"From the trash in front of a crook's house," Spade replied. "The goon works for one of the gangs, and this character has a bad memory. He writes a lot of stuff down."

Tommy was clearly impressed. "So, this is how you get scoops for the show?"

"It's one way. But, I don't announce anything without corroboration. I have other sources."

"Wow! How did you learn all this, Mr. Spade?"

Al Spade's reaction surprised the youth. Spade paused and his expression grew wistful. He stared out the window without actually seeing anything. "In another life, kid" he said, his voice barely a whisper. "In another place."

"Tommy!" Ross's voice boomed through the offices. "Where is that kid?"

Spade snapped out of his reverie and smiled at Tommy, "You'd better go. Mr. Ross needs you."

After the boy had gone, Spade shrugged into his overcoat and left his office.

On the way to the elevators, he passed Maybell who didn't see him at first, then called him back. "That was a really terrific report Mr. Spade," she said, beaming.

"Oh, uh thanks Maybell," Spade replied, distracted. "Was there some-thing you wanted?"

"Yes! I have a message for you. It came while you were on the air. It's from Mr. Aaron Agnew. He wants you to call him today."

Spade glanced at his watch. "I'm swimming in it at the moment. But Aaron's an old friend of the family. He knew my folks well. I'll see what I can do. Thanks, Maybell."

Spade found a pay phone in the lobby and piled inside, closing the door behind him. Coins clinked and numbers whirred. The phone was picked up on the first ring.

"Hello, Uncle Aaron," Spade said, pleasantly. "I got your message. What's up?"

Agnew's voice rattled excitedly over the line, "I had a visit today from a couple of toughs shilling a protection racket. They tried to put a scare into me."

Spade's face darkened and he squeezed the handset in his fist. All business now, his tone betrayed concern. "Are you all right? They didn't hurt you, did they?"

"No, no, I'm fine. I agreed to pay and told them to come back tomorrow at closing time."

Spade's voice was cold as ice. "Do you want me to be there?"

Aaron says, "Not at all. You're not a cop anymore, my boy. Don't worry, I have my own plans for them. Just wanted you to know you might have something good for that show of yours."

•••

Later that evening, a small two-story building with a barber shop on the ground floor seemed to be attracting the attention of the ragged men and women shambling by. The shop was dark and appeared shut up but the furtive passersby were drawn to a side door. The people, nervous and fidgety, traipsed in and out.

Inside, the back of the shop contained a counter with a metal gate. The customers slid soiled bills through the gate to a man who handed out a small kit then thumbed the buyer to one of the empty cubicles lining the walls. Each was furnished with a ratty cot and small table. A drape on a horizontal pole could be drawn like a shroud across the opening. The customer, tall and emaciated though bearing the ghost of a once strong physique, shook in anticipation as he clutched his kit to his chest. The kit contained a hypodermic needle, spoon, matches, rubber tubing, and a packet of heroin.

The man at the counter did not give the customer a second glance. The hophead was just another in a long line over the course of many long nights. The counter man thrust his calloused hand forward to take the meager life savings of the next in line. At that moment a loud crash vibrated the entire building.

The stunned counterman shifted his beady eyes to the door as it burst inward. An apparition in crimson stalked across the threshold, a strange looking gun in each hand.

"Everyone out of here!" the new arrival bellowed. "This den will be splinters in one minute! Get out now!"

The Red Badge punctuated his words with a series of shots. Glass shattered. Screams tore the somnolent silence.

The counterman attempted to aim an automatic, but a snapped shot from the Red Badge found the mark and the weapon tumbled from numb fingers.

Heads popped out of the cubicles, slack faces grinned in ecstasy or stared open-mouthed in disoriented wonderment. The last druggie to score stormed out and rushed the man in red. "It took me all day to get enough for my fix you – "

The Badge holstered his guns and flipped the man onto his back on the filthy floor.

"You'd better get out while you can, or you'll die for your habit."

He picked up the stunned junkie and pushed him through the smoking entryway, then checked each cubicle in turn, pulling dazed and delirious stragglers out and pushing them towards the exit. Satisfied the place was deserted, the Red Badge began tossing small bombs behind him. Pausing as if considering, he finally grabbed up the counterman and pushed him out the door, placing a red badge in his hand.

The Red Badge barreled through the milling, dazed crowd and brought his motorcycle to life. Without so much as a glance over his shoulder he rode away as the first of a series of explosions rocked the night behind him.

•••

Spade was at his desk, banging out the day's copy with the first coffee of the day sitting stone cold at his elbow when Ross appeared in the doorway. "Al, Mr. Harris wants us, right away."

Spade finished the sentence he was working on, then rose up out of his seat and threw on his jacket. It was not good policy to keep the owner of the station waiting. He joined Ross in the hallway. "Any idea what he wants?" Spade asked as they approached the elevators.

Ross shook his head. "Not a clue."

Getting out of the elevator onto the 21st floor, the two men walked to the corner office. The pretty, blonde secretary greeted them with a dazzling smile and jabbed the intercom to announce their arrival. She rose gracefully out of her chair and conducted them through the oaken doors to a large sumptuously furnished office, the grandeur of which was obscured by the excessive amount of clutter. The large cherry wood desktop was covered by a half dozen telephones and papers strewn all around. Two large leather chairs faced the desk.

Seated at the desk was Steven Harris, fifty years old, impeccably dressed and trim in an expensively tailored dark blue shirt with a red and blue striped tie. His wavy, graying hair was impeccable. Harris had launched KACM himself ten years before, and was now the sole owner of a small chain of fifteen such stations throughout the mid-west. Of which KACM was the flagship. With the sleeves rolled up on his sinewy forearms, and a constant fire in his eyes, Harris looked ready to double that number.

"Ah, boys, come in, sit down," he said in his deep baritone. "I'm sure you're wondering why I called you up here."

The men sat and gave him expectant looks.

"I have three pieces of business," Harris went on. "The first is to compliment you, Al, on your reports. You're doing great, and it's garnering us a lot of interest and listeners. We're even getting some new sponsors. Fat cats."

Spade crossed his legs. "That's good to hear, Mr. Harris. I'm trying to put these crooks out of business. If we make money on it, all the better."

"And I want you to continue doing it, Al. I want you to keep pushing. But that brings us to our second piece of business. The station is being pressured to either rein you in or fire you. Most of the noise is being made by Kuark, the Mayor, and some members of the city council. But a couple of smaller, local, sponsors have closed their accounts with us, and have told me, flat out, that they'll reconsider if I fire you. I told them what they could do with their concerns. Now, what I want you to do is step on the gas. You're hitting nerves so keep it up. Pull out all the stops!"

Harris's mood changed as he considered how to broach the third item of business. "All right, now we all understand each other. High ratings are one thing but I'll not see a good man risk his life without doing something about it. Al, there have been death threats and I'm concerned for your safety. You're taking potshots at scum with long histories of hitting back. When I think of what happened to your sister – "

Al's face reddened. His lips twisted and writhed as though a primal scream of rage threatened to burst from his lips. "I'll get whoever was responsible!" he hissed. "Do you hear? If I have to bring every racket down with my bare hands!"

A look of genuine concern on his face, Harris watched helplessly as his employee and friend grappled with his demons. "Al, calm down. I understand your feelings, and I'll do whatever I can to help you find the SOBs. I only mentioned it because the gangs in this town will stop at nothing. Right now you're doing a splendid job of making things tough for them. The public has become more vocal, demanding the police and the mayor do something about the crime rate. The murder of that little girl the other day has fanned the flames. You know people have been coming into the lobby to leave money for the girl's family! We had to set up collection baskets. Good, decent folks leaving quarters, dimes, nickels, pennies – whatever they can spare. We've collected over $700 so far. All because you publicized it on your broadcast. You're doing good things here. Because of that, you and this Red Badge character are at the top of every hit list in town. With you tearing a strip off Carbone during the day and the Red Badge blowing his businesses all to hell at night, Boss Carbone has got it in for both of you. And the other gangs must be getting plenty nervous thinking they may be next. Look, they don't know who the Red Badge is and they can't find him. But they can find you. That's why I don't want you going anywhere alone. I want you to use Walter York as a bodyguard."

His emotions in check, Al thought for a moment, then shook his head. "No, I can't do my job if he's around me all the time. One glance at an ex-cop dogging my heels and my sources will dry up. No one will talk. Plus they'll think I've got a yellow streak and can't stomach a fight." Spade paused before continuing. "You know, it wouldn't be a bad thing if Sarah had someone to watch over her though. When Bronson or I aren't with her."

"That's not a bad idea, Steve," Ross spoke for the first time. "The scum of this city might get it into their heads to finish what they started."

"It would put my mind at ease, sir," Spade added.

Harris realized he would get no further with his stubborn star. "All right," he said. "But Al, be careful out there."

•••

The factory was unremarkable from the outside. Just one of many that made up the backbone of Central City's industrial district along the riverbank. In this particular factory a light burned in one window, keeping the darkness at bay. On the other side of the streaked, grimy glass lay a large room divided down the middle by diverse apparatus. One side of the expanse was filled with laboratory equipment: arrays of chemicals on shelves along with vats, centrifuges and mixing chambers. The other half of the room was taken up with metalworking machinery, lathes and buffers. At a table a man worked in a lab coat, mixing liquids in beakers. He scribbled cryptic entries in the notebook beside him.

The man was not alone in the room. A stout woman of middle-age, wrapped in a shawl against the weather outside collected her purse and gloves from a locker before addressing the man in heavily accented English. "Mr. Mays, I'm a-leaving now."

"What?" His concentration broken, Bronson Mays looked up at the woman. "Oh, Mrs. Balboa. Is it six o'clock already?"

"All-a-most sir." She observed him as he bent over his work again and took a step towards him. "You should be a-going, too. You should a-look in on that a-poor Miss Sarah."

Mays's shoulders slumped and a look of despair played across his handsome features. He shut his green eyes tightly and rubbed at them with the thumb and forefinger of one hand. Blinking back the fatigue, he raised the hand and slicked back his sandy brown hair.

"I'll be leaving directly, Mrs. Balboa. Just have to clean up some stuff. Don't let me keep you. I'll see you tomorrow."

"Yes sir, see a-you tomorrow." With a sad shake of her head, Mrs. Balboa turned and walked out of the factory/lab.

Bronson returned to his work, mixing chemicals, heating beakers on Bunsen burners, and making notes, the lateness of the hour forgotten. An unexpected sound behind him made him turn. Three hulking men were standing there.

"I'm sorry," said a man wearing a leather jacket, "but no one answered our knock and the door was unlocked. I hope you don't mind our coming in."

One of the toughs behind the leather jacket spoke up, "Do you want I should lock the door, Alberti?"

"No, Luigi. We're fine."

"If you don't mind, gentlemen," Bronson began, interrupting the exchange. "I'm busy and the factory is closed for the day, as are our offices. Whatever your business is it'll have to wait until tomorrow."

"I'm afraid our business can't wait," Alberti replied with feigned regret. "We noticed there's a large warehouse connected to the factory building here. We're going to rent it."

Mays put his pencil down and turned to face the men. "It's not available to rent. Look, I'm sorry you came out here for nothing. Now, if you'll excuse me, I have work to do and someone I need to see, so please leave."

Alberti stepped forward and towered over Mays. "I don't think you understand. Your warehouse is perfect for our needs and we mean to have it. We'll pay you twice the asking price."

"A generous offer, but one I'll have to decline. Now, please – "

One of the other men joined Alberti, encircling Bronson. A little shorter than Bronson's own six feet, but wider and thicker, with arms as big around at the bicep as some peoples' thighs, the goon threw a sudden punch at Bronson's stomach, but staggered off balance as the blow missed completely. Bronson had moved deftly to his left and was behind the man in an instant. Bronson caught the man off balance, shoving the thug hard in the back. The man's head struck a glancing blow against the lab table and he was knocked senseless.

"Not bad," Alberti said, approvingly. "But can you stop … wha …?"

As Alberti pulled a revolver, Bronson Mays darted quickly to the man's right, grasped the gun hand, twisting it downward and disarmed him, then pulled up sharply, pressing the empty hand between Alberti's shoulder blades. Mays spun Alberti around, using him as a shield against the third thug.

"Stay right there," Mays cautioned. "I'll drop you where you stand, then take your boss's arm off at the shoulder and beat the both of you with the wet end."

The thug, unused to acting without orders shrugged his shoulder helplessly and stared at Alberti, "Boss, you want I should take this guy?"

"No! Don't move, you idiot."

Bronson smiled without humor. "Smart boy. All right, listen and listen good. I'm not renting the warehouse. Not now, not ever, and certainly not to scum like you or the reptile you represent. Don't think of coming back or next time I won't go so easy on you. Understand?"

Alberti winced as Bronson yanked the pinned arm higher. "I, ugh, understand. Now you gotta understand, my boss ain't gonna like this, and my boss always gets what he wants."

"Well, I guess there's a first time for everything." Bronson released his captive and pushed him toward the goon. He covered the two men with the revolver. "Pick up your garbage and get out."

The two men hauled the dazed man off the floor and, supporting him, the trio staggered out of the factory.

•••

Aaron Agnew watched the hands of the clock over the shop door as they crept inexorably towards the hour of six p.m. The hour struck with a delicate series of chimes from the antique clocks scattered about the shop. These soft tones were followed by the jangle of the bell over the door as two rough looking men entered. One of them was familiar to Agnew, being the man who had pushed the radio to the floor the day before. The second was a stranger, but cut from the same cloth as the first.

The first man, his name was Jacks, stalked to the counter and leaned across it to glare at Agnew. "Where's the money, mac?"

Agnew remained stoic, asking, "Where's your friend with the fedora?"

"He's the front man," Jacks explained. "We do the collectin'. So, where is it?"

Suddenly the two henchmen heard four strange squealing retorts outside.

The man at the door stood up straight, his eyes wide as he caught his partner's eye. "Hey, Jacks, ain't that the sound Curly and Moe said the Red Badge's heaters make?"

"Yeah, Blackie." Jacks turned back to Agnew and grabbed him by the collar, "You didn't get the Red Badge here to gun us, did you?"

"How would I know how to contact him? I'm willing to pay your blood money to keep trouble away."

Jacks shoved Aaron back roughly, then turned to Blackie. "Let's get outside and see if we can spot him. If he got Carlo and Russo collectin' across the street, maybe he don't know about us and we can get the drop on him."

Over his shoulder, Blackie cautioned Agnew. "You stay here. When we finish with the Badge we'll be back for the moolah."

Both men drew their guns and sidled to the door. Blackie crouched and peered past the drawn shade. Convinced the coast was clear, he nodded as much to Jacks and the two men barreled out into the street. They managed two rapid steps when an odd twanging sound reached their ears. Suddenly Jacks felt a sharp prick in the back of his left knee. As he fell face first into the street, the sound came again and he saw a scarlet knife appear in the back of Blackie's right knee.

As the two men writhed and moaned a paper wrapped object landed in their midst. Through the pain Jacks stared at the item through slitted yes. A gust of wind unfurled one corner of the paper, revealing a red badge.

Agnew observed this scene from the doorway, a strangely shaped crossbow in his hands. Storing the crossbow into a special compartment in the counter, Agnew picked up the phone and called the police.

Fifteen minutes later ambulance attendants were tending to the injured, thrashing, yelling men while Agnew finished his account to a police officer of what had transpired. "There were a couple of low squeaking noises and the next thing I knew, they were on the ground. I saw a man in red, with a wide-brimmed hat, then he was gone. I don't know what else I can tell you."

The officer closed his pad and regarded Agnew frankly. "Thank you, sir. You may have spotted the Red Badge in action. You're a lucky man. These two are part of Boss Carbone's gang and that's trouble you don't want."

•••

The midnight stillness of Central City was characterized by an eerie calm, like that tranquil instant before an explosion. The pawn shop appeared closed from the front but a light burned in a back room at that late hour. With no hint of an approach, the side door which gave on the back room suddenly burst open and several small spheres flew through the doorway to clatter and roll on the floor. They immediately spewed dense red smoke, filling the room. A short rat-faced man wearing a stained shirt and a green visor coughed at his desk. His tearing, watering eyes glimpsed a tall man dressed in dark red emerging out of the cloud, pointing a strange looking gun.

"Come out from behind there!" the figure in red barked.

Cowering, the man opened the cage and stood facing the Red Badge, his hands raised.

"No games and you'll live longer," the Red Badge continued. "I know this is Carbone's fencing operation and you're his paymaster. Give me your keys and get out."

"The boss will have my hide if he thinks I helped you," the man spluttered.

"Do you think I give a damn? Hand them over."

"Here, here!" The quavering man reached down, then gave his shirt cuff a shake. A knife dropped into his waiting hand and he lunged at the stomach of the Red Badge. The man in red was quicker. He formed an 'X' with his wrists and blocked the thrust, then jerked his arms to his left, twisting the knife hand until the blade fell. Continuing the motion, the Red Badge yanked the man's arm at an unnatural angle until the shoulder dislocated.

As the small man screamed in agony, his knees buckling, the Badge searched his pockets and pulled out a ring of keys. He stuck the keys in front of the man's wide, staring eyes. "Which one?"

"The gold one," the man gasped. "There's a compartment."

"I know." The Badge kicked him in the direction of the front door.

Striding quickly behind the counter, the man in red kicked open a false panel and quickly unlocked the exposed drawer. The drawer contained valuable jewels Carbone had ordered put aside for his personal inspection before being fenced lest he wish to bestow them as gifts to his many lady friends. The Red Badge pawed through the items and his grasping fingers finally landed on a sparkling necklace and brooch. Pocketing these, he pulled out several black balls from the folds of his scarlet duster. These he armed, then threw behind him as he dashed for the front door.

There were mere seconds before the grenades exploded and the Badge sought to use that time to put some distance between him and the doomed building. However he managed only a few hasty steps when he was suddenly struck across his masked face. He staggered but did not fall.

As stars danced before his eyes, the Red Badge heard the strained voice of the shopkeeper who had regained his bravado. "Get him Buck! Look what he did to me!"

Momentarily blinded, the Badge was not defenseless. He used his forward momentum to blunt Buck's next blow while continuing his forward motion. Twisting to the right like a jungle cat to face his attacker, he weaved and blocked ferocious blows while his senses returned. His vision cleared at last and he seized the wrist of the oncoming arm and twisted clockwise before striking the right elbow with his palm, breaking his assailant's limb. He lashed out with his foot and connected soundly with Buck's right knee, eliciting a scream as the ligaments tore. Buck dropped as though pole axed and the Badge slashed across with the flat of his hand to the man's throat, laying him out.

The Red Badge's eyes bore into the rat-faced shopkeeper. The man's grip on his dislocated arm tightened, then he turned and ran.

As the Badge silently moved away on his cycle, the pawn shop exploded with a thunderous crash and a wave of heat like the devil's hand shoved between his shoulder blades. The cycle swerved but held the road. The work of the Red Badge was not completed this night. Keeping to side streets and alleys, he threaded his way deeper into the underbelly of the city. His destination was a condemned building on the east side where he'd learned a secret meeting of a sizable portion of Carbone's gang was to take place. The cycle stopped silently near a grime-smeared window. The Badge dismounted and peered through the opaque glass. Harsh, agitated voices reached his ears from a dozen men clustered in a tight group, gesticulating wildly as they bickered. There would soon be peace in that room, and corpses. The Red Badge pulled his guns and strode towards the black maw of the open doorway. Beneath his mask, he smiled.

•••

As the Badge silently moved away on his cycle, the pawn shop exploded with a thunderous crash.

The papers reported little else the next morning and even a special edition could not satisfy the curiosity of a galvanized society. The name of the Red Badge was on everyone's lips as Central City dealt with the aftermath of the swath of justice the man in red had cut through the underworld while the city slept. Al Spade reporting what had been accomplished the night before spoke with wonder in his voice as he read the report.

"Citizens of Central City, we have a savior in our midst. It's about time someone stood up to the scum of this city and delivered a message that is long, long overdue. Last night the Red Badge struck blows against the Carbone mob which all but brought that nest of vipers down. Like a surgeon operating on a cancer, the Red Badge first shut down Carbone's insurance racket near Somerset Park. Next stop was a pawn shop long suspected of being a fencing operation of Carbone's and, it turns out, the main payroll office for his goon squad. The bank is closed, mooks! And the crime concern you've sold your souls to is soon to be out of business.

"But the Badge saved the best for last. Before the dust could settle on the ruins of Carbone's stolen treasury, the police responded to a call at a condemned building on the east side. The reports I've received say it resembled a battlefield of the Great War. A dozen men lay sprawled on the floor, all dead from gunshot wounds. Rumor has it a red badge was found at the scene – our savior's calling card.

"The police will not confirm that these incidents are the work of the Red Badge. They claim the knives, even the badges found at the scenes, were all made of some strange plastic which melted hours after being retrieved.

"However, we know the truth! Don't we folks? Ladies and gentlemen, let's call a spade a spade, the Red Badge's methods may seem cruel, but he's up against harsh and brutal men who have inflicted nothing but death, pain and fear on you, the citizens of this city. Not one innocent has been harmed in the Badge's attacks. I'm sure I speak for all of us when I say I feel safer walking the streets of the city I hold dear. Perhaps the day will come when we might all sleep soundly in our beds once more."

•••

"How the hell is he doing it?" Bruno Carbone smashed his fists down on the desk of a foreman's office he'd claimed for his own. His voice echoed through the vast expanse of a bankrupt cannery near the pier. "How does this bastard know where to hit us? How did he know about the warehouse? The gambling joint and the pawn shop?"

The gathered men hung their heads like condemned prisoners. No one could look his fellow in the eye. All eyes avoiding meeting those of Carbone or Batelli.

Carbone caught their hang dog expressions. "Don't nobody go soft on me! This Red Badge clown got his licks in but we're not on the mat yet." He pulled a .45 from his waistband and pumped a round into the chamber. "Anyone looking to take a powder on me, just say the word and I'll send you on your way. Am I making myself clear?"

Carbone's threat shook the men from their despondent misery. They raised their heads and squared their shoulders. Carbone liked what he saw. "All right, then. Now, like I was saying, we need to find out how the Badge is getting his info."

"We don't know, Boss," Luigi, one of Carbone's top lieutenant's replied. "He's taking us apart a piece at a time."

"If there's a leak, I pay you crumbs to plug it, don't I?" Carbone observed.

Ricci seated beside Luigi spoke next. "We're tight as a drum. I'll stake my rep on that. But the Red Badge keeps hitting us where it hurts. And we don't have enough manpower left to cover what's left."

Carbone's expression darkened. "Yeah, especially after that slaughterhouse on the east side. The Badge actually did me a favor on that one. I know a Judas council when I see one and those yellow rats were going to leave me twisting in the wind. I got tipped and me and some boys were heading over there when the Badge hit the place and wiped the lot out for us. Too bad he didn't stick around so I could thank him properly."

Carbone's bravado emboldened what was left of his gang. He had their attention again and now it was time to remind them who was running the show. He pushed back from the desk and strode purposefully around the room. "OK, we're going to pull back on everything for the next couple of days," he began. "Everything is closed. All of it."

"But boss, the marks will go to the competition," Ricci complained. "We can't let that happen."

Carbone smiled devilishly. "Ricci, you worry too much. Don't you get it? We're losing money now with this mook tearing down everything we sweated years to build. The thing is, he can't hit what he can't find. So we shut up tight. Since you mugs can't find him, we'll take away his targets and draw him out. Trap him. Now do what I told you so we can finish this clown and get back to business."

The meeting broke up. The lieutenants moved quickly to the exit, their steps purposeful once more, their black souls once more committed to personal gain through the exploitation of the helpless. "Batelli, Alberti," Carbone called to the retreating backs of his closest lieutenants. "Hang back a minute. I need you to do something."

•••

Twilight's shroud had just settled over Central City and the Mays Metal and Plastics factory was quiet. Inside Bronson Mays worked in his laboratory unaware of the close of another day. Suddenly a loud crash resounded through the building as the main entrance was smashed down by a large, heavy truck. Several men erupted from the back of the truck while more strode into the shop through the smashed doorway.

Alberti and 'Bat' Batelli emerged from the truck. Carbone's chief enforcer receded into the shadows Alberti boldly moving forward while the rest of the gang gathered in front of the truck.

"Mays!" Alberti bellowed.

Bronson turned from his work and faced the men. "Alberti. Back for more, huh? Here to make another offer on the warehouse?"

Alberti's black eyes blazed. "No offer this time. We're taking the place. You should have played ball when you had the chance. Now we get to make an example of you."

"If you handle me the way you've handled the Red Badge, I've got no worries."

Alberti and Batelli both became enraged at this jibe. Alberti lips twisted cruelly. "Take him down!"

The gangsters broke their ragged formation and surged forward. Mays paused a moment and then flicked a switch on his lab table. A metal net dropped and covered the onrushing crew. Alberti, who had been close behind the group leaped back in time. Batelli receded deeper into the shadows. While the gunsels thrashed under the net, Bronson stabbed a button, and an electrical crackle filled the musty air. The covered men stiffened under the net which began to vibrate. The trapped goons shuddered, their limbs jerking spasmodically. Bronson again fingered a button and an eerie quiet pervaded the room. The men lay still. An acrid odor filled the warehouse.

Alberti looked on in astonishment.

"They're not dead," Bronson explained. "Although they could well be, if I chose. I only used enough juice to stun them. They'll be alright until the police arrive."

Alberti had had enough. He pulled his gun and hurled hot lead at Bronson Mays.

The slug from Alberti's gun stopped bare inches from Mays's breast. The bullet hung in the air, which seemed spider-webbed with cracks. Alberti stared dumbfounded.

"Like it?" asked Bronson. "It's a new type of plastic shield I've been tinkering with."

Alberti fired again, uselessly. Further slugs struck the plastic pane only to be caught suspended in the invisible barrier.

'Bat' Batelli chose this moment to strike. He stalked around the invisible barrier, and swung his weapon.

Bronson ducked under the powerful swing, the bat passed over his head so closely that it lightly brushed his hair before smacking against the wall. Bronson lashed out, driving a fist into Batelli's stomach, forcing him to retreat a couple of steps. In this brief respite, Bronson Mays spied the weapon in his attacker's hand.

"A bat! You're the one!"

With a primal growl, Mays leaped at Batelli, who swung again, missing cleanly, though driving Mays back. Emboldened, Batelli swung the bat in great sweeping arcs, preventing Mays from closing, forcing him to retreat until his back pressed against the lab table. Alberti danced around, trying to get a clean shot at Mays but Batelli was in the way.

With a triumphant glint in his eyes, Batelli paused. "I don't know who you think I am, but it doesn't matter now. I'm going for the home run."

"And here's the pitch!" Mays fumbled behind him, grabbed a beaker of liquid, and threw it at Batelli's head. The enforcer dodged the missile, but not the liquid contained in the beaker sloshing out onto his suit coat. The fabric began to smolder. Momentarily startled by this attack, Batelli's swing lost its power and the bat struck Mays only a glancing blow. Seizing his advantage, Mays moved forward and caught Batelli's arm and, using Batelli's own momentum against him, flipped him heavily to the floor, wresting the bat out of his grasp in the same fluid movement.

Batelli sprawled stunned on the floor, looking up as Mays prepared to pound him with his own weapon. At that moment Alberti, who had reloaded his revolver, came around the plastic obstacle and took aim at Mays.

Reacting on pure instinct, Mays hurled the wooden shaft at Alberti. The bat clipped the right side of Alberti's head, felling him.

Mays whirled to finish Batelli with his bare hands, but the hitman had scrambled out the open door. In the distance police sirens could be heard drawing closer.

•••

The Red Badge's arrival at the south side pier went unnoticed. He stalked quietly toward the docked cargo ship, his dark red garb blending into the shadows created by the weak moonlight cascading down on the warehouses, squat office buildings and the draped pallets offloaded from the ship. The figures atop the buildings watching with binoculars escaped his notice. One man standing watch on top of a warehouse penciled a beam of light at the wheelhouse of the docked ship.

Bruno Carbone, caught the signal and turned to a rough-looking gunsel. "Mickey, he's coming. His escape route is plugged. When I give the signal, fire the flare. While the boys are closing in, we'll hit the spot. That'll light him up good."

"Yes sir."

Steadily the Red Badge closely approached the gangplank, his eyes darting for danger lurking in the nearby shadows. Suddenly the sky lit up with a million sparks. A flare! Looking hurriedly away lest his night vision be obliterated in the bright light, the Badge was suddenly illuminated head to toe by a high-powered spotlight which turned night into day. Guns chattered and bullets tore up the planking at his feet, whipped through his scarlet cloak and whizzed by his ears. A shot flung his broad-brimmed hat to the pier, exposing a head completely covered in red fabric with only openings for his eyes.

In one fluid movement, the Badge threw himself to one side while digging into the pockets of his garments. Several small spheres appeared in his red-gloved fist. These he scattered about him. They exploded with muffled puffs and a dense scarlet cloud quickly enveloped the wharf.

The raging gunfire continued. The gang fired blindly into the crimson smoke as they attempted to tighten the noose.

Those closest to the cloud faintly heard a low, telltale squealing.

Shadows once more took possession of the pier as the shattered spotlight rained scalding fragments down on the gunmen. The men hesitated.

"Keep firing!" Carbone yelled from his place of safety. "Watch he doesn't come out of that smoke."

Gunfire continued as the breeze off the water dispelled the smoke. The men found two of their number out of action, then cast their glances about in search of a sprawled bullet-ridden crimson-clad corpse. They didn't find it. Nor did they find any blood traces. Only a crimson hat bobbed in the gently swelling waves.

The Red Badge had disappeared.

•••

"Citizen of Central City," Al Spade spoke somberly into the microphone clutched in his fist. "You've all heard by now about the arrests at Mays Metal and Plastics last night. You may have read that several members of Bruno Carbone's mob were arrested at the scene with firearms on their persons. You may have delighted at hearing that Carlo Alberti, a top lieutenant of Carbone's, was also taken into custody at the factory. The charge facing the lot: attempted robbery. However, what you may not know is that the sordid bunch, including Alberti, were granted bail and are back out on the streets of this fair city."

"How much longer are we going to stand for this corruption, ladies and gentlemen? How much longer will we sit idly by while Carbone tucks a once proud police force and justice system deeper into his back pocket? The word out of Captain Kuark's office is that there was insufficient evidence to hold the men despite the statement of Bronson Mays himself!

"And where were the police while gunsels shot up the pier hours later? What happened to the night watch? Where were the beat cops? Kuark sites a scheduling error as the cause, but we know differently, don't we citizens? And what of this: a dark red hat was found at the scene – a hat bearing a striking resemblance to that reportedly worn by the Red Badge. The police will say no more. And no further sightings of the Badge were reported last night."

"Calling a spade a spade, there was no scheduling mistake. Carbone needed the slip cleared of police and that's exactly what he got, courtesy of Kuark's office. Perhaps a trap had been laid for the Red Badge. And, at this moment, no one can say whether or not Carbone's plan succeeded. Have we seen the last of the Red Badge? Are the scourges of our city celebrating their victory right at this very moment?"

•••

Tommy Balboa was never happier to see the lights of home. The coldwater flat in one of Central City's roughest neighborhoods resembled a palace after the day he'd had at the station. Al Spade's broadcast had touched off a powder keg. The phone operators had been swamped with calls as people demanded information on the Red Badge. Tommy had been run off his feet ferrying messages to Mr. Ross and Mr. Harris from the sponsors calling in with their concerns. The Police Commissioner threatened legal action if a public apology was not issued immediately to the CCPD.

The sun had just set and the streetlights whirred to life, taking up their battle to dispel the darkness as Tommy mounted the steps to his front door. He could only shake his head in wonder at the chaos of the afternoon and ponder whether or not things would ever settle down, if the citizens of Central City would one day live in peace once more. He stepped through the open door and hung his coat and cap on the hall rack and ran a hand through his black hair. "Mama, I'm home!"

"Tomasino, is that you?" his mother called from the kitchen in Italian. "You're late. Go wash up. Dinner's ready. We have a guest today."

Tommy Balboa walked deeper into the small apartment, but did not see a visitor in the living room or parlor. Confused, he shuffled to the kitchen to speak to his mother. He crossed the threshold and stopped abruptly.

After a moment, "Hello, sir," he said to the visitor seated at the table across from his mother.

"Why so formal, Tommy?" Bruno Carbone asked. "Come give your Uncle Bruno a hug."

Tommy reluctantly did so then moved to stand between Carbone and his mother at the stove.

"So, Tommy, tell me," Carbone began, his eyes never leaving the boy's. "How's that job at the radio station?"

●●●

The next morning, Tommy Balboa paused in the open door of Al Spade's office, then knocked meekly on the frame. "Mr. Spade, you got more letters here," he stammered. "Do you want them now, or should I put them on your desk?"

"The desk, kid. I'll try to get to them later."

Tommy placed the bundle on the desk, then headed for the door. He hesitated a moment before turning back to Al Spade. "You know, Mr. Spade, folks would like to know more about the Red Badge. You sometimes interview people on your show, like the Mayor, Captain Kuark and them others. How come you don't talk to the Red Badge?"

Spade looked up from his work and stared off wistfully for a moment. "Now, there's a great idea, Tommy. If I could find him, that is. And get him to agree to an interview." Al thought for a minute then snapped his fingers, saying, "I think I know a way. You'll get full credit for the angle if I can pull it off – maybe even a bonus as well."

Minutes later, Spade was in Ross's office. "What's up, Al?" Ross said, not looking up from the papers on his desk. "Make it quick. We're still putting out fires here after that bombshell you dropped yesterday."

"Just following orders from up top, Herm," Spade replied. "Okay, here's what I've got in the hopper. Tommy had this idea I do an interview with the Red Badge."

Looking up from his desk, "Say, I like that," Ross admitted.

"So do I. Problem is, how do we contact him? We don't even know if he's still alive.

So how about this? In today's broadcast, I invite the Red Badge to do an interview. We'd have to agree on a secure location, no cops. We'll let him tell his side of the story, find out why he's got it in for Carbone. What do you think?"

"What do I think? I think you should be revising your copy right about now to include that invitation. This is genius! Where will you meet?"

"Easy, I'll leave it up to him. We'll set up a private telephone line for him to call, one that doesn't go through the switchboard, but directly to my office."

"I'll have it ready before you go on the air."

News of the coming announcement spread like wildfire around the offices of KACM and a palpable tension filled the office as Al Spade closed the door of his broadcast booth.

"This is Al Spade for radio station KACM. Before we get to the regular business of calling a spade a spade today, I have an announcement. If you can hear me Red Badge, I'm offering you a chance to speak directly to the people of Central City. I want to interview you. You pick the time and place. No cops. And I'll come alone. We've set up a special private telephone line to my office. The number is Keystone-2233. That's Keystone-2233. The citizens of Central City want to kynow what's driving you. What are your plans? Whose side are you on? So, call me at the conclusion of this broadcast and you can set the record straight."

After the show, Al Spade and Herman Ross were huddled over the telephone in Spade's office.

"It's been an hour since the broadcast ended," Ross observed.

"We're not sunk yet."

"Yeah? What if he doesn't call? This thing could backfire on us."

Spade ran his hands through his hair. "Herm, you're making me nervous. Get out of here. I promised the guy privacy, remember?"

"All right, all right, I'm going." Ross rose from his chair and had just closed the office door behind him when he heard the telephone jangle. His hand still on the doorknob, he opened it a crack and shot a silent question at Spade who had the handset pressed to his ear. Spade caught the gesture and nodded quickly at Ross.

"Yes, this is Al Spade," Spade barked into the receiver. "You want to get your story out? Okay, just tell me where and when." Spade made a thumbs-up gesture to Ross who closed the door behind him. Spade scribbled something down on the pad near the phone, in his eagerness he pressed down so hard on the pencil that the lead snapped as he finished writing. He hung up the phone and ripped the sheet from the pad.

Spade sprinted to the door and dashed up the aisle between the desks. Tommy, lingering nearby, stuck his head into the empty office, his eyes on the pad by the phone.

•••

An hour later a silent crimson motorcycle turned off the main highway and glided up the dirt road leading to an abandoned farm on the northern outskirts of the city. The cycle slid to a halt behind a copse of alders a short distance from a large barn. A scarlet figure rose from the seat to blend with the darkness.

Inside the sagging structure, hidden behind moldy hay bales, Bruno Carbone waited, his ears straining for any sound of his approaching prey. The wind was rising, rattling the trees and sounds echoed off the rough walls around him. He bent to peer through a crack in the warped boards when all of a sudden, from the loft above, a board creaked.

Carbone spun and stared mutely as a figure seemed to manifest itself from the night. It stepped from the edge of the loft and landed gracefully before the gang boss.

"Bruno Carbone," the Red Badge said. "Uncle to Tommy Balboa, a page at the KACM radio station. And owner of this farm you no doubt swindled from your grandfather."

Bruno Carbone stepped out from behind the hay, "You know a lot about me, yet you set up the meet with Spade here. In a place I own? Big mistake."

"You concealed seven gunsels in and around this barn. They have been taken care of."

"All seven, huh? And where is Spade?"

"I intercepted him on the road and turned him back. I knew you were planning to kill him, too. I could not allow that to happen."

"All right, what now? You gonna take me down once and for all?" Carbone crossed his arms. "Thing is, I like even numbers. There weren't seven of my men here, there were ten. You missed three. Get him boys!"

The quiet barn erupted in gunfire as men boiled out of their hiding places. One of the men blasted with his .45 while another sprayed the room with hot lead from the tommy gun in his fists. Shotgun blasts punched holes in the wood and the wind entering through the smoking maws in the wall, stirring up wood splinters and strands of hay which reduced visibility in the darkened barn to almost nothing.

The Red Badge suffered direct hits in the opening seconds of the attack, falling backwards while bullets whizzed over his head and kicked up the earth around him.

Thinking the battle won, Carbone shouted his victory over the din from the firearms. "Thought you could get the drop on me! I'm no penny ante mug! There better be enough left of you for me to finish off, personally. Boys! Knock it off with them guns!"

The firing ceased and Carbone moved gingerly toward the spot where the Badge had fallen. Carbone's men joined him, pressing closer, guns at the ready. There lay the Red Badge flat on his back, unmoving. The men observed the impacts on the Badge's crimson coat where their bullets had found the mark and silently congratulated themselves. Carbone tuned out their chatter as his gaze roved over the fallen form. There was something about the downed Badge that was not quite right, but he couldn't put his finger on it.

Then he had it. There was no blood!

Carbone dove to one side just as the fallen man raised his guns and the squealing hiss of the strange weapons' fire reverberated through the barn. The surprised gunmen jerked and stiffened before they were felled by the deadly fire.

The Red Badge was on his feet in an instant, pointing both barrels at the sprawled Carbone.

"It's down to this now, huh?" Carbone said, breathing heavily, his homburg tumbled from his head. "Let me tell you one thing before you pull that trigger. I never was any good at math. I didn't bring ten guys with me. I brought eleven."

"I know." The Red Badge dove forward as a shuffle of shoe leather announced 'Bat' Batelli's entry into the battle. The baseball bat struck the Badge in the back and he pitched forward. His leap had lessened the impact of the blow, otherwise it would have shattered his spine. However it was powerful enough to disarm him. Rolling forward with the momentum of his dive, the Badge came smoothly to his feet, facing Batelli.

"Did you think I'd believe for a second you'd go anywhere without your lapdog, Carbone? I was counting on his presence tonight. That your favorite bat, Batelli?" The Red Badge screamed at Batelli "The one you used on a defenseless woman after you raped her! Is that the bat you used to cripple her before leaving her for dead?"

"Nah," Batelli replied, offhand. "It's the one I'm gonna use to cave your head in!"

The berserk man in red threw himself at Batelli. The enforcer was ready for the charge and drove one end of the bat deeply into the gut of the Red Badge. The blow sent the Badge reeling backwards. Sensing victory, Batelli rushed in, the bat tracing deadly arcs as he closed.

However the Red Badge was not as incapacitated by the blow as Batelli believed. The scarlet avenger had feigned injury to bring Batelli closer. The Badge dodged the swooping bat and launched himself under the arm's backswing. Trapping the hand with the bat between his own arm and side, the Badge drove two numbing jabs into Batelli's ribs. Air whooshed out of the enforcer's puffed cheeks and the man bent slightly at the waist. Like a crimson tornado, the Badge pounded a third jab to his opponent's nose which crunched under the impact. Three more piston-like blows pummeled Batelli's gut and solar plexus. The Red Badge released Batelli, left the man staggering – the bat still held tight in his fist.

"Not so much fun when your victims fight back, is it?" the Badge asked. "You're not facing a woman in terror now. You're facing the end, Batelli!"

Batelli screamed his rage, swinging wildly. The Red Badge stepped lithely to his right and struck Batelli in the left wrist with a precise chop. Batelli's wrist bent at an unnatural angle from the blow and there was a loud, satisfying, snapping sound. Nerveless fingers released the bat which clattered to the earthen floor.

Picking up the fallen weapon the man in red systematically battered the fallen enforcer. First he broke the man's arms at the elbows, then the left knee was caved in. Batelli fell in a heap. His rage overcame the agony and Batelli struggled to rise to his feet.

The Red Badge stared down at the groaning man. "And now for the home run stroke!" With all the strength he could muster, the Red Badge whipped the bat into Batelli's bleeding face with a two-fisted swing, laying him out for good.

The Red Badge hurled the bat through one of the remaining windows and turned

*"You're not facing a woman in terror now. You're facing the **end,** Batelli!"*

to face Carbone, standing in frozen shock, fearing the next minute.

The Red Badge jabbed a crimson finger at Carbone, "You ordered it done!"

The accusation shook Carbone from his trance. He pulled out a revolver and pointed it at the man in front of him. "Stay away! I'll shoot you, stay away… "

One scarlet arm whipped like a snake. This motion followed by a thin, whizzing red streak towards Carbone and suddenly the hand holding the gun was impaled with a slim crimson blade. The gun fell to the floor as Carbone clutched the injured hand to his chest.

Carbone shrieked as he backed away. The Badge closed in. "No, please!" the crime boss pleaded. "I'll give you anything you want! Don't – "

Striding forward, the Red Badge said, "The great, terrible Bruno Carbone, pissing in his pants and begging for his life. But before we put you out of your misery, there's someone who wants to say something."

At a gesture from the Badge, Tommy Balboa walked out of the shadows. "Uncle Bruno."

Carbone's smiled his relief at the sight of a friendly face but the smile lasted only an instant when he grasped the meaning of Balboa's presence at the farm. "You helped him do this to me, Tommy? You would do this to the family?"

Tommy took an enraged step forward, his fists balled at his side. "Don't speak to me of family. You killed papa!"

"You got it wrong. It was one of the other gangs. I didn't kill your father. Why would I do that to my sister's husband?"

"You did it because he wouldn't join your outfit. Papa wanted honest work. I was in the closet when you came to him with 'one last chance.' To help you rob the bank where he worked as a guard. I saw you! Through a crack in the door, I saw you! You become angry when papa said no. I saw you shoot him!"

Tommy turned to the Red Badge who had regained his weapons. "Give me your gun!" the boy wailed, tears in his eyes. "Let me finish him!"

The Red Badge holstered his weapons., and spoke softly, "No, Tommy. You have to leave now. He will be punished, but I won't let you do it. You're nothing like him, kid. You're a good boy who'll grow up to be a good man. If you do this it will haunt you the rest of your days. Go home, take care of your mother."

A tearful Tommy Balboa glared back at Bruno Carbone, then spat at the gangster. "So long as he is punished for what he did."

"You have my word," the Red Badge assured the youth. "Look at him. Defeated, his gang destroyed… You heard him beg for his life. This is the fate of all men of low character. Remember!"

Tommy left the barn and the Red Badge regarded the gangster boss, "For all the lives you destroyed, for all the crimes you committed and ordered done, there's nothing left for you. Nothing except this!"

The arm of the Red Badge flicked again and a second shiny crimson streak closed the distance between the two men. The stiletto blade embedded itself in Carbone's throat. The red handle instantly lost in the blood pouring from the wound. Carbone dropped to his knees and then toppled face first to the floor.

"You will never destroy another innocent," the Red Badge said to the twitching form at his feet. "You will never prey on the vulnerable again. You will die alone as all men of your ilk do in the end."

The man in red turned and strode out the door.

•••

"That material inside the coat worked wonders, Aaron," the Red Badge said as he slid the garment from his muscled shoulders. "The shotgun pellets and bullets didn't penetrate. They hit like a swarm of sledge hammers, but that's all."

The two men were in the basement of Agnew's fix-it shop. The old root cellar had been converted into an amazing laboratory lit by overhead fluorescent lights. A work table was heaped with gadgets in various stages of completion. Shelves of spare parts lined one wall.

The Badge hung the coat on a peg near the table and stripped off the scarlet suit coat.

"The coat stopping a shotgun blast and the bullets … oh, ye of little faith. It caught those slugs at the pier."

"Easy to say when you don't have to wear the thing and the guns are pointed at you," the Badge chuckled. He hung up the coat and was removing his red shirt revealing the white undershirt below it.

Agnew smiled at the comment, but his tone grew instantly serious. "So, is it over? Can we have peace at last after what happened to Sarah?"

The Badge paused in donning his dress shirt. "For now." He turned and met Agnew's gaze. "But, I've got to continue, Aaron. There are more gangs out there and this city needs to be cleaned up."

"Let the police handle it, my boy," Agnew implored, trying to read the expression that went with the piercing eyes but the red mask was still in place.

"There is too much corruption on the force. You know that. But it's not about that. There are other victims, like Sarah. Who will fight for them? Who will keep evil from visiting their doorsteps? The Red Badge has more work to do. And so do you. That is, if you want to continue helping me."

The wizened old man sighed. "Very well. I will continue to help in my small way. If only to keep you alive and eventually talk some sense into that thick skull of yours."

"Is that any way to talk to me?" the Red Badge was fumbling at the mask obscuring his face. He pulled it off at last and faced Agnew.

"Like they say on the radio, just calling a spade a spade," Agnew replied, cryptically.

•••

The small clapboard house was like many in this quiet part of town. Al Spade climbed the stairs and opened the door of the house he had grown up in.

"Sarah, I'm home!" he called. "Are you ready for some dinner? How about spaghetti with marinara sauce?"

Wheels creaked on the wooden floor as a wheelchair being pushed by Walter York entered the hall. In the chair was a young woman whose striking beauty was marred by a sagging of the left side of her face and the yellow ghosts of healing bruises. "I'd pre'fr mc an chee," Sarah said, her words slurred by the nerve damage to her face. She tossed her head to sweep back a lock of chestnut hair which had fallen across her good auburn eye. The other still puffed shut.

"Ok, mac and cheese it is." Spade leaned forward and kissed the top of his sister's head. Then he straightened and addressed York. "Will you stay for dinner Walter?"

"No, thank you, Al," the tall, blocky, ex-cop said, shaking his large head with its sparse salt and pepper close-cropped hair. "Have to get home to the missus. She hates it when I miss dinner."

"Maybe next time, then. Thanks for looking after Sarah."

"No thanks necessary. I don't mind watching her. But, I think she cheats at checkers." He added a wink for Spade's benefit. Spade saw him out, then joined Sarah in the kitchen.

The water had just begun to boil on the stove when the doorbell rang. Spade walked over and opened the door. "Hello Bronson. I thought you'd be here when I got home."

Bronson Mays walked in with a familiarity born of experience. "I was working late at the factory. Developing some new plastics. Fantastic properties. I ran samples over to Aaron."

"Sounds good. I'm sure they'll be put to good use." Spade glanced down at Bronson Mays' coat pocket and spied a small bulge. His tone softened. "You still carry it around, don't you?"

Mays hung his head for a moment, then met Spade's gaze and there was the fire of determination behind his eyes. "I'll carry it until the day Sarah gets better and says yes."

Spade leaned in towards Mays and whispered so Sarah couldn't hear. "That's a day Central City will see sooner rather than later, my friend – if the Red Badge has anything to say about it!" Then in a normal tone he continued, cordially. "I'm making dinner, Bronson. Sarah wants mac and cheese. Interested?"

Red is for Rage

Red Badge was born on a train.

I like riding the trains. I like to fly too (mostly in open cockpit biplanes. Flying in a jet is too much like a bus. A flying bus). However, I hate the time in the terminal, the undressing for security (take off the belt and the shoes), don't bring in any bottles full of liquid (I finally figured out I could bring empty bottles and then fill them with water inside. Save myself lots of money buying the overpriced water in the terminal. Ha). You know, the hassle.

But trains, comfortable seats, electrical outlet to plug in my laptop, I can walk around, there's a food cart (if I forget to bring some sandwiches) and no distractions–like TV or radio or Internet. I can work or read or sleep during the relaxing trip. Yes, it takes longer, but I like it. It's also cheaper, generally.

I was returning home from the Windy City Pulp Convention at the end of April 2010 where I'd seen Ron Fortier and Rob Davis at the Airship 27 table. Ron had told me they were doing something new. They were going to start publishing new, creator-owned, pulp characters in a new anthology titled 'Mystery Men'. Understand, I'd been collecting pulp magazines for a long time, and comic books. My favorite comic characters are The Batman and Green Lantern (both influenced by pulps, mind you). My favorite pulp characters are The Shadow, Secret Agent X, the Black Bat, Operator #5 (pre-Purple War), and the Spider. I like and collect most of the pulp hero characters and other pulps as well. I'd been trying to get into writing, and writing for the Airship, for a while, but my writing had problems. Nice ideas and plots, but the writing …

So, first I slept, or tried to, on the train, and then an idea formed. And then the idea just shot out. I couldn't contain it. It was screaming, "*Let me out. Let me out.*" I was typing on my laptop as quickly as I could. IT JUST WOULDN'T STOP! The hero would be dressed all in red, with a western influence. He'd have these cool, semi-silenced guns, and he'd also throw knives, and his calling card would be a red police style badge. Oh, and the red badges and knives would eventually melt. I was off and running.

In the course of my trip home I created the bible (a compendium of characters, weapons, situations, locations) for the character. And then the first short story. A 5,000 word story. I was literally typing "The End" as the train arrived at Penn Station in New York City.

Before emailing the bible and story to Ron I polished it up a bit. Then waited for his response. A couple of weeks later Ron replied. Loved the bible. Add 10,000 words to the story. So, over the next two weeks I added, and edited, and added, and edited.

Then sent it in. As before, this needed polish. So, Andrew Salmon and I collaborated on the novelette and, Andrew did a great job in polishing me up.

What you've read is that story.

Now, don't ask who Red Badge is. I'm not saying. That will come out in a future story or two or three. You'll have to wait. After all, the anthology is titled 'Mystery Men' and that's the mystery. Who is Red Badge? I enjoyed writing it. Hope you enjoyed reading it. I'm looking forward to your comments, good (I hope) and bad (well, hope not too many).

Oh, and look to http://red-badge.com for further info on the Red Badge.

•••

MARK S. HALEGUA -The late Mark Steven Halegua was born in Fairbanks, Alaska on an Air Force base. He graduated York College with a degree in English, then went into computers, where he was an IT Consultant since (that's Information Technology, not "cousin It!"). He loved to read, and collected comics and pulps for quite a while (turns out, collecting pulps before he even knew what they were). He proudly had complete sets of Phantom Detective, Black Bat, Startling Stories, and Captain Future in original pulp, just to list a few. Some of his favorite current authors are David Weber, Jim Butcher, F. Paul Wilson, John Ringo, and Kyle Mills. Mark was a much-beloved friend of the publishers and is missed.

The Red Badge was his first published fiction. His character creation, The Blue Light is being shepherded by Nancy Hansen and Lee Houston and should see publication from Airship 27 in the near future.

•••

ANDREW SALMON - is a two-time Pulp Factory Award nominee, and won the award for his first Sherlock Holmes story, "The Adventure of the Locked Room" (*Sherlock Holmes Consulting Detective: Volume One*). He is also a Pulp Ark Award nominee and has been nominated for an Arthur Ellis Award (the equivalent of the Edgar) in his native Canada. His work has appeared in numerous magazines, including *Masked Gun Mystery, Planetary Stories, Parsec, Storyteller, TBT* and *Thirteen Stories.*

He is creating a Brand/X superhero serial novel currently running in *A Thousand Faces Magazine.*

He has published or appeared in fourteen books: *The Forty Club* (which Midwest Book Reviews calls "a good solid little tale you will definitely carry with you for the rest of your life"), *The Light Of Men*, which has been called "a book of such immense significance that it is not only meant to be read, but also to be experienced... a work of grim power" – C. Saunders. *Secret Agent X: Volume One* and *Three, Ghost Squad:*

Rise of the Black Legion (with Ron Fortier), *Jim Anthony Super Detective: Volume One, Sherlock Holmes Consulting Detective: Volumes One, Two* and *Three, Dan Fowler G-Man: Volume One, Black Bat Mystery: Volume One, Mars McCoy Space Ranger Volume One, The Dark Land* ("a straight out science-fiction thriller that fires on all cylinders" – Pulp Fiction Reviews) and *Mystery Men: Volume Two (with Mark Halegua)* constitute his work for Airship 27 to date. Andrew's work will also appear in the upcoming *The Moon Man Volume One* and Rick Ruby anthologies from Airship 27 as well as many other projects in various stages of development.

To learn more about his work check out the following links:
http://www.amazon.com/Andrew-Salmon/e/B002NS5KR0/ref=ntt_athr_dp_pel_pop_2.
www.airship27hangar.com
www.lulu.com/AndrewSalmon
www.lulu.com/thousand-faces

Jack Minch
ACE REPORTER

"Lair of the Mole People"
By Gregory Bastianelli

Reporter Jack Minch sat at his desk in the newsroom at the New York City paper staring at the empty seat at the desk opposite his and began to worry. It had been more than a week. He opened his bottom right drawer and withdrew the sealed envelope. He turned it over in his sweaty hands a couple times, then stopped and stared at the neat printing on the front:

IN CASE I GO MISSING

Lavonne Valliere had given him the letter with strict instructions not to open it unless she hadn't returned in seven days. This was the eighth day, and Jack wondered if she meant if she didn't return on the seventh day, or after seven days. *Had he waited one day too long?* He hoped not for her sake. He looked at the clock on the wall, then back at the empty chair. At one minute past the hour she normally showed up at work, never not on time, Jack tore open the envelope and began reading the note inside.

Lavonne hadn't told him anything about where she was going or what she was doing. It was a "secret assignment" she had said. Not even Bob Murray, the paper's city editor, knew what it was.

Now, Jack Minch read her note. She said she was researching a story about the people who, rumor had it, lived in the abandoned tunnels and sewer and subway lines beneath the city. Many of them had been forced out of their homes during the Great Depression and driven underground out of desperation. Legend referred to them as the "Mole People." Lavonne said she had found a contact who could lead her to a long abandoned passage, and she planned to descend into this underworld and find the people who inhabited it. She wanted someone to know where she was, in case she didn't return. The name of her contact was listed, and there was a crudely drawn map.

Jack leaned back in his chair after finishing the note. He had heard about the so-called Mole People, sure everyone in the city had. It was a myth, though. No one really believed there was a society of people living underground. But Lavonne apparently did. And now she had gone down there.

Jack cursed himself for following her instructions to wait a week. He should have opened the letter right away, and then maybe he could have stopped her before she left on this foolish mission. Now, who knows what's happened to her down there.

Sure, there were abandoned subway tunnels and such, probably miles of them beneath the city. But the only inhabitants down there were crazed vagrants and hobos. And he could only imagine what they would do to a beautiful woman like Lavonne Valliere.

Damn her!

He jumped up from his seat. He had to talk to Murray.

•••

They sat in the office of the publisher, Harrison G. Swanson, on the top floor of the building. Murray and Minch seated before the great wide oak desk covered in sheets of paper, photographs and stacks of newspapers. The larger figure of Harrison G. Swanson leaned back in his chair. He twisted one end of his thick gray handlebar mustache. Two bulging eyeballs stared back at them from the large head with the receding hairline above the never-ending forehead. On the wall behind the high-backed chair hung an African shield, a short spear, a pair of tribal masks and a bullwhip, souvenirs from a trip abroad. On either side of the desk were two large potted yucca plants.

It was quite impressive. In the years he'd worked here, Jack had never been in the publisher's office. None of the reporters had. They weren't important enough. Murray was always the buffer between the publisher and the staff.

"Sure she came in here a little over a week ago," Swanson said in a booming voice as if he were talking to a big audience. "Wanted paid time off to pursue some cock and bull story about underground people living in a city beneath the city."

"I don't know why she didn't talk to me about it," Murray said, shaking his head, sounding dejected he hadn't been consulted by reporter or publisher. "She should have come to me first." He was aggravated. He hated reporters doing things behind his back, out of his control.

"Oh, she was all excited about it, but wanted to keep it a big secret." Swanson said. "Said she didn't want anyone to know she was working on the story."

"So what did you tell her, sir?" Minch piped in, leaning forward in his chair, feeling antsy.

"Told her hell no!" He waved a dismissive hand. "Said it was a wild goose chase. I wasn't going to give her paid leave to spend a week traipsing around subway tunnels looking for a nonexistent society of cave dwellers. Waste of money and time. We pay her to work on real stories."

"Well," Murray said. "That story has been around a long time."

"Urban myth!" Swanson yelled, banging his fist on the table. "Nothing but a dumb legend. End of story. That's what I told her."

"Well it wasn't the end for her," Minch said. "She went after it."

"Yes," Murray said. "She came to me and asked to use some of her vacation time. Took the whole damn week off."

"And now she hasn't returned," Minch said, shaking his head, wondering what mess of trouble Lavonne had gotten herself into.

"Well, her vacation is over, and she's not back." Swanson said, sitting up straight. "If she isn't back in the next two days, she's fired. End of story."

Minch and Murray exchanged glances. Would Swanson really do that? Minch wondered. Valliere was one of the paper's best reporters.

"Should I write something about her disappearance, get the word out. Talk to the police?" Minch asked.

"What for?" Swanson asked.

"She's a missing person. It's a crime story. I've got the crime beat."

"She's just a reporter who didn't show up for work." Swanson said. "That's not a crime."

"She's a well-known person who's disappeared in the city, sir," Murray exclaimed.

"She's just a reporter, not a celebrity," he bellowed. "Nothing goes in the paper."

"Then let me go looking for her sir," Minch implored.

"Out of the question!" Swanson banged his fist on the table. "I need you here writing crime stories. That's what sells newspapers, not some story about people living in tunnels."

"But she probably needs help."

"Then she shouldn't have gone." He glared at the two of them. "I don't need two AWOL reporters. End of story!"

Jack Minch was angry as he left the publisher's office with Murray.

"We've got to do something," Jack said, steamed.

"You heard Swanson," Murray replied, shaking his head. "End of story."

"I don't care what he said." Jack grabbed his arm and waved Lavonne's letter in his face. "She asked for someone to come looking for her. And that's what I'm going to do." He turned and stormed off.

"But you don't have any time off coming to you," Murray yelled after him.

"Then fire me!"

•••

The office of Detective Mike Emerson in the 17th Precinct was tiny and dark. The dim bulb overhead cast most of the room in shadows. Minch sat across from Emerson's desk, smoking a cigarette. The detective did likewise and the smoke floated upwards toward the slowly spinning ceiling fan which then dispersed the plume into wispy tendrils that scattered around the room.

Minch didn't really want to get fired. He liked his job too much. Writing about robberies and bank heists, kidnappings and murder. He lived and breathed the crime beat. That's why he came to the 17th precinct. If he could get Detective Emerson to investigate Lavonne's disappearance, then it would be a legitimate crime story and the paper couldn't ignore that. Not even Harrison G. Swanson.

Detective Emerson was the right person to come to with this case. He was one of Jack's best contacts in the police department. They had bonded over being ex-military men, Jack with the Marines and Emerson with the Army. The two of them had been too young for the Great War and regaled about the heroic stories of the soldiers, like Blackjack Pershing, Sgt. York, Private Murphy and the Fighting 69th.

But there was another reason Jack chose to come here. Emerson had long had a thing for Lavonne Valliere. Heck, who didn't. She was beautiful, with long thick black hair that cascaded down over her shoulders in waves. And a knockout hourglass figure. Minch had long thought about trying to cross the line of friendship and co-workers, and attempt something more.

But who was he kidding? Jack was no pretty boy. He had a flattened nose from his boxing days in the Marines, as well as red crew cut hair and freckles, along with pale skin that didn't handle the sun too well. And sun was something Lavonne cherished.

The office of Detective Mike Emerson in the 17th Precinct was tiny and dark.

She was well-tanned and loved going to the beach. She liked to hobnob with a lot of the celebrities she did profile pieces on and often hung out at some of the exclusive beach resorts on Long Island.

Jack didn't go anywhere near the beach and kept out of the sun as much as possible. It just made him sweaty and pink. And some of the classy people she brushed elbows with, well, Jack wasn't exactly their type of people. That's why she was a feature writer, and he was just a beat hack. He wrote about stabbings and shootings, mobsters and bank heists, the dark ugly side of life in the city. He feasted on the crime and the grime with a hunger. Lavonne found the excitement in the city. Whether it was landing with the passengers of a dirigible after a trans-Atlantic voyage, or waiting at the top of the Empire State building to interview the daredevil who had just scaled the skyscraper, Lavonne always managed to find the heartbeat of the city.

But Lavonne Valliere was no glamour girl, and neither Jack nor Emerson was surprised to hear she went down into the tunnels after a story. She was trading the heartbeat of the city for a journey into its bowels. She always knew how to find a good story. Or often, a good story would find her. But now it was up to them to find her, before it was too late.

"Nasty place down there," the cop said. "Don't know if there are really Mole People living in a society, but there are sure some dregs of the city hanging out about down there. Wackos and street thugs. Even the cops are afraid to venture too far down."

"But not you, right," Jack said, leaning forward and blowing out a puff of smoke.

Emerson sat straight up in his chair, throwing back his shoulders.

"I remember years ago," he said, taking a long drag on a cigarette. "I was just a beat cop. I had to accompany some detectives down into the tunnels. That was back when they were working on the big expansion project, before it got shut down by the Depression." He took another drag and blew out a plume of smoke that drifted upwards. "Back then, they had a lot of the tunnel workers actually living in the tunnel work areas in little brick shacks they built for them. They would spend weeks at a time." He caught Jack's eyes. "That's a long time to be underground. It seems one of the workers went stir crazy. Attacked his co-workers with a pick-ax. Killed them all but one. The wounded man managed to crawl up to the surface to get help." He paused and took a deep breath. "We went down there and found a slaughterhouse. Bodies and blood everywhere. The killer had run off into the tunnels. We searched for a while, but never found him. He just disappeared into the tunnels." Emerson sucked another drag into his lungs. "Who knows, maybe he's still down there after all this time. Crazy scary place down there. I swore I'd never go down there again." He shivered.

"We're talking about Lavonne Valliere" Jack said. "She's worth it, isn't she?"

"Hate to think of a dame like her down there." He shook his head. "Who knows what someone could do to her."

Jack held up the note she had left.

"I have her contact right here," he said, waving the piece of paper. "What do you say we head down after her? The sooner the better."

The detective rubbed his chin.

"Could be a little too late."

"I'm going with or without you," Jack said. "And I'd rather have you with me."

The detective took a small flask out of his bottom right drawer, unscrewed the cap and took a swig. He handed it to Jack.

"Let's go."

•••

The three men stood over the open grate on Second Avenue as morning mist rose up around them. Jack Minch stared down into the opening, like looking into the maw of some carnivorous beast. And they were about to descend into it. A metal ladder descended into the opening. He glanced up at Mike Emerson with a smirk, and then looked at the third man.

That man was Hank Barnes, a transit worker in his late fifties.

"Before the Depression," Barnes said, "The City Council approved the building of the Second Avenue subway line. They even had a ground-breaking ceremony in one of the tunnels." He sighed. "Then when the stock market crashed, the bottom fell out, and the project stopped. All the work that had been done was halted."

He pointed at the opening beneath the metal grate he had lifted up. "This here leads to one of the service tunnels that had been prepared. There are three stations that had been built, but never finished. The tunnels were cut under most of Second Avenue before the work stopped. They were temporarily sealed up. A connector with Grand Central was built, but then also sealed up when the project was halted. This is the way I led Miss Valliere in."

He shook his head.

"I warned her, Mr. Minch," Barnes continued. "I been working in these tunnels for about thirty years. There are places down there you just don't want to go."

"People really live down there?" Emerson asked.

Barnes nodded. "Mostly 'ics.'"

Minch looked confused.

"Addicts, alcoholics and psychotics. Some street gangs use the tunnels for hangouts. It's a nasty place down there. They come up to forage or rob every now and then. Some never surface." He shook his head again. "Nasty place."

"No use wasting time," Jack said.

Mike nodded and handed him an electric torch.

"Okay," he said. "I'll be right behind you."

Jack grimaced as they descended the rungs of the metal ladder into the world beneath the city.

The darkness enveloped them immediately and they turned on their torches. It was damp and dirty, the air thick and musty. Their footsteps echoed on the cement floor as Barnes led them down a narrow corridor. The walls seeped with moisture. Jack felt like he was in the throat of some sleeping beast.

They came to a T-juncture and Barnes stopped. Jack flashed his light down to the left, then right. Both were long endless tunnels, larger than the corridor they had just come from.

"This way," Barnes said, signaling to the right.

They jumped down onto the floor of the tunnel. Jack scanned his light across the rounded ceiling as the walked. It looked pretty stable. They plodded on in silence for several minutes, the only sound their echoing footsteps. Every now and then Jack would hear a scampering sound.

"Track rats," Barnes said. "They grow pretty big down here."

Jack flashed his light around the edges of the tunnel, but didn't see anything.

"I hear some of the people down here trap them, then cook them over a fire and eat them," Barnes said.

"Yummy," Mike Emerson said.

"Better they eat them, than you," Barnes countered.

"Just delicious," Jack said. What kind of nightmare were they walking into?

After about twenty minutes of walking, the tunnel opened up wide, with a platform on the right. They climbed up a set of steps to the elevated platform.

"This here would have been Jackson Station," Barnes said.

Jack flashed his light onto the back wall, and saw it was tiled.

"You have your map?" Barnes asked. Jack pulled it out, waving it in front of him. "Good, cause this is as far as I go."

"What?" Emerson said.

"You won't catch me anywhere near where you're going. Sorry. I hope you find Miss Valliere, she was a real nice lady. But this ain't no place for a lady. Or even for us."

He turned and began walking back the way they had just come.

"Thanks a lot," Jack said, sarcastically.

"Good luck," Barnes hollered back, his voice echoing through the tunnel. "I'm sure you're going to need it."

They watched as his light grew fainter down the tunnel, and then disappeared all together. Jack shivered in the silence. Even with Mike Emerson, he felt alone. He looked at Mike, then down at the map in his hand.

He pointed his torch down the tunnel before them.

"That way?" Mike asked.

"You got it."

They walked down the long dark tunnel for what seemed like an hour. They barely said a word to each other the whole time. For some reason, Jack felt they should be quiet, as if he were afraid of being noticed, though anyone could see them coming from the lights they shined to illuminate their path. He wished they could turn them off, but knew they would be immersed in total darkness, blind as a bat.

Every now and then they could hear a distance rumble of one of the subway lines. Sometimes it came from their left, sometimes from below, eventually it only came from above. How many levels of tunnels were there, he wondered? How deep did it go? It was as if they were in a giant labyrinth. Rats in a maze, looking for the cheese. Or cheesecake in this instance. How could Lavonne have come down here? Looking for some prize-winning story no doubt. What in the hell was that girl thinking?

They heard a sound and both stopped. It was a snorting sound.

"What's that?" Mike whispered.

"It sounds familiar," Jack whispered back.

They stepped forward slowly, and the sound grew louder. They stopped and flashed their lights around.

One beam caught a bundled mass up against the tunnel wall on the right. It slowly heaved up and down. They cautiously moved toward it.

It was a body.

It looked like a pile of dirty laundry, but there was actually the shape of a man in it. Their light grazed a weathered grimy face with a matted beard. The man was asleep on a filthy mattress and snoring. Garbage was strewn around him.

"Should we wake him?" Mike asked.

"What the hell for?"

"Ask if he's seen a woman poking around down here. Maybe she interviewed him."

"I can't imagine what she would have gotten out of this guy."

They stared at him a second longer, then decided to continue without disturbing him.

The tunnel forked and they followed the right side which supposedly would lead to another abandoned station. The ground sloped and Jack felt they were descending deeper into the earth. He found it amazing that the city could stand above all these tunnels, wondering why the whole metropolis didn't just cave in.

They continued down the tunnel 'til they reached some steps that led to the abandoned station. They flashed their electric torch lights around. Another abandoned subway station. Tiles covered the wall behind them, but then ended abruptly in a jagged edge, like a partially completed jigsaw puzzle. This station had never been finished.

"Just think," Mike said. "All the money the city spent building this, all the work, time and effort, and for what? To just let it sit empty."

"What a waste," Jack said looking around, imagining the amount of workers it took to construct this, wondering how they felt when they walked off the job, never to return. At the far end of the station was what looked like a brick cabin, with glassless windows. "What's that?"

Mike followed the light of his torch and gazed upon the brick structure.

"That looks like one of the temporary bunkhouses they built for the workers building the tunnels, so they could stay down here for days on end."

They came up to the structure and Jack peered in one of the windows. He wondered if the crazy pick-ax killer might be still living here, maybe in this very structure.

"God, what a way to make a living," he said. He shone his light inside.

"Get that outta my face," yelled someone, and Jack saw a body stirring on a mattress.

"Jesus!" Jack exclaimed. "There's somebody in here."

The man got up off the mattress.

"Of course there's somebody in here! I live here dammit! Who the hell are you?"

The man's face was grimy and he wore dingy overalls over a plaid flannel shirt.

"Yeah," came a voice behind them. "Who the hell are you?"

Jack and Mike spun around and their lights caught two more figures behind them, two thin men, one wearing a long gray duster, the other a black bowler on his head. Something clicked and flashed and Jack saw the man in the duster had a switchblade in his right hand.

"We're not looking for trouble," Jack said. "We've just got some personal business down here." Jack and Mike backed away from the brick cabin a few steps.

"Oh no," the man with the knife said. "That's where you're terribly mistaken." He waved the knife around. "You have absolutely no business down here."

The man in the bowler hat grinned, a toothless smile.

"You see," he said. "This is our home." He pointed to the cabin. "And you'd be trespassing."

The man in the overalls came out of the cabin to their left, and Jack saw he was tall and had broad shoulders.

"And we don't take kindly to strangers," the bowler man continued. "Especially ones traipsing around where they don't belong."

"Then we'll just be on our way," Jack said, backing up a few steps.

The man in the duster laughed. "That's not how it works down here," he said when he finally stopped. He continued to slowly weave the knife through the air, back and forth, menacingly. "There's a price to pay for trespassing."

Jack looked at Mike, who met his gaze.

"I got you," Jack said, and slowly reached into his back pocket and removed his wallet.

The duster man laughed even harder.

"No, you don't got me," he said. "What we want is what you're wearing."

"Sorry," Mike said. "Don't think my pants are quite your size." He looked at the big man in the overalls.

"We're not asking," bowler man said. "Drop your duds, now." Duster man took a step forward, knife out in front of him.

"Easy," Jack said, backing away slowly.

Mike turned to look at Jack. "It's okay," he said, winking. "I think we understand what these gentlemen want." He started to pull off his jacket, and then quickly whipped out his service revolver. "I'm a cop, you thugs!" he said, training the gun back and forth on the three of them. Jack could see the wide expressions on their faces. "Now back up, all of you." He looked at the big man who moved over toward the other two.

"Now now," the duster man said. "Don't get jumpy."

"Put the knife down and back away," Mike said.

The duster man placed the knife down in front of him, and then the three of them took several steps back.

"Get the knife, Jack."

Jack ran forward, grabbed the knife off the ground without taking his eyes off the three men, and then ran back to Mike's side.

"Turn around," Mike said, "and start walking."

The three did as they were told, walking along the platform till they disappeared into the darkness. Finally a voice came from the blackness where Jack had last seen them.

"You're going to need more than that gun down here, copper."

The last syllable of the last word echoed along the cavern walls.

"Let's go," Mike whispered.

Jack slipped the knife into his pocket and they turned and continued out of the station and down the tunnel path.

Jack was worried the three men would come back; maybe take some other tunnel and come out in front of them, and maybe bring some friends. He was glad he was with Mike. And he felt a little better having the knife.

They continued on their journey in silence.

At one point, Jack could hear the sound of dripping water. He scanned his torch overhead and saw pipes running along the sides of the tunnel near the ceiling. One of them was leaking, the drops forming a small puddle on the ground. The drops splashed and echoed throughout the chamber.

"Wait," Mike said, grabbing his shirt.

"What's the matter?"

"Turn your light off."

They both did and the world suddenly turned black. Jack never felt so alone in his life. Even though he knew Mike was standing right beside him, knew he could reach out and touch him, he could not see him or anything else. It was as if he were struck blind. He had no idea it could be this dark.

"I thought I saw something," Mike whispered and it startled Jack because the words seemed to come out of nowhere.

"What was it," he whispered back to nothing.

"Something moving."

"Well, we won't be able to see it if we keep our lights off."

"But then, it will see us."

"Maybe it already has."

"You're right."

That didn't sound like Mike. Jack was startled. In fact, he knew Mike was beside him, and that sounded like it come from behind them.

"Did you say that," Mike whispered.

"No," Jack said.

"I did," came the voice from behind them.

Jack didn't know what to do. Turn his light on? Run? Scream?

"Who are you?" Jack finally asked.

"Who are you?" the voice asked back.

"I'm a police detective," Mike answered. "And I have a gun."

Great, Jack thought. Thanks for warning him.

"What do you want?" the voice asked.

"We're looking for someone," Jack said. "A woman. A reporter."

"Lavonne Valliere?" the voice asked.

Jack spun around. "You know her?" He turned his light on.

Nobody was there.

Mike turned his light on and they flashed their beams around.

"Where are you?" Jack screamed and his echo screamed right back at him.

"Over here," finally came an answer from deeper down the tunnel.

They couldn't see anybody, but hurriedly followed the sound of the voice. They moved so quickly, Jack didn't notice till the last second that a thin string stretched out in front of them just inches above the ground. It caught their ankles and they both tumbled forward to the ground. Just as quickly, a large heavy net dropped down on top of them. Suddenly several pairs of arms had grabbed a hold of them.

•••

They were blindfolded and had their hands tied behind their backs before being marched for what seemed like more than an hour. Hands guided them through twists and turns, their path always seemed to be descending. Their lights, the knife and Mike's gun had been confiscated. Their captors would not speak to them, so they trudged along in silence, stumbling every now and then, but their handlers wouldn't let them fall.

Suddenly, even through the dark blindfolds, they sensed brightness. Jack wondered if they had been led back to the surface, because it felt like light was shining down on them. But no, that couldn't be. He had sensed, even sightless, that they had been going down, not up.

They were stopped and hands quickly removed their bindings and blindfolds.

There was bright light, shining down from above. But it wasn't the sun. There was a great spotlight high up on a ceiling. They were in some great cavern and Jack looked around. There were buildings, or rather, things that resembled buildings, lining both sides of the cavern. Jack saw men, women and children standing outside the buildings, frozen in silence, staring at him and Mike like intruders, which he began to realize they were.

A booming voice came from atop a set of concrete steps to the right.

"Welcome," said the voice of a large barrel-chested man with a dark beard. He raised his hands. "Welcome to Twilight City."

Jack looked all around him and saw people began to mill about, no longer interested in the new visitors. The structures lining both sides of the cavern walls looked like little cottages with flat roofs. But there were no doors or windows, just openings. The dwellings all bore fresh coats of bright colored paint.

The bearded man came down the steps that descended from a large stone structure.

He approached them and Jack could see the man was in his late fifties, maybe early sixties. There were streaks of gray in his dark beard. The man extended a large meaty hand.

Jack took it, hesitantly. The grip was firm but friendly.

"Who are you?" Mike asked.

"My name is Professor Theodore Titus. I am the commissioner of Twilight City."

"What is this place?" Jack asked, as the man shook Mike's hand.

"This is our community," he answered.

"They had weapons," said the man they'd encountered in the tunnel. He handed the knife and gun over to the commissioner, who looked at it with disapproving eyes. He glanced at both of them.

"Thank you Max," he said to the man before turning back to them. "Weapons are not allowed in Twilight City," he said sternly.

"My name is Detective Mike Emerson, New York City Police Department, and I'm authorized to carry a gun anywhere in New York City."

The commissioner tsked and shook his head.

"This is not New York City," he said. "We have our own laws down here. I'm afraid we'll have to hold on to this for you."

Mike started to step forward, but Jack stuck his arm out and held him back. Now was not the time to try and start trouble. The commissioner looked at him.

"And you?" Titus asked. "A cop as well?"

"No. My name's Jack Minch. I'm a reporter."

The commissioner rolled his eyes.

"Not another," he said.

Jack's eyes widened.

"They say they're looking for Lavonne Valliere," Max said.

"Have you seen her?" Jack asked, excited.

The commissioner looked puzzled.

"Has she not returned to the surface?"

Jack shook his head. "She's been gone over a week."

"Oh my goodness," the commissioner said, his brow furrowed. "That's not good." He stared down at the ground for a moment, deep in thought, and then looked up at Jack. "Come with me."

They followed the commissioner up the steps to the large stone structure. At the top, Jack looked down and realized this looked like a little town.

Once inside, they sat at a long rectangular table. The commissioner and two others sat in three high-back chairs. Jack and Mike Emerson sat across from them in smaller chairs.

"This is The Meeting House," the commissioner said. "We hold all our commission meetings here and make most of our important community decisions."

"And Lavonne Valliere's been here, you said." Jack was antsy.

The commissioner sighed. "Yes. She came down here, looking to verify the rumors of an underground society. She wanted to write a feature about our lifestyle. I was quite reluctant to let her stay, but she's very persuasive."

Jack smiled. "She sure is." Who could resist helping such a sweet-talking dame?

"We let her stay with us for a few days. She saw how we lived, talked to several of the inhabitants, learned about our culture."

"How do you live down here?" Detective Emerson asked.

"We have all the amenities we need," the commissioner said, sternly. "Our

"This is The Meeting House," the commissioner said.

inhabitants consist of all members of society, like you above. We have our teachers, doctors, artists, plumbers, carpenters, electricians." He looked at Emerson. "Even policemen." He nodded to Max beside him, who grinned. "We live a full life down here. Our children attend school. Everyone works to contribute to the community. We have tapped into power lines to obtain electricity. We've connected to water lines for hot and cold running water."

"So you're stealing utilities," Emerson said.

"We prefer to think of it as sharing. Our whole society is based on sharing down here. Our food, our necessities. Nobody has anything that someone else doesn't have."

"Sounds kind of fascist to me," Emerson said.

"We think of it more as a communal society. Everybody benefits. As a result, we have no crime down here."

"Then why do you need a policeman?" Jack asked.

"That's more because of outsiders," Max piped in, "like yourself."

"And Ms. Valliere?" Mike asked.

"We welcomed her," the commissioner answered, "and she lived among us."

"She always believed in the existence of you people," Jack stated. "The Mole People."

The commissioner's face drooped.

"That's where you're quite mistaken Mr. Minch." He shook his head. "We're not the Mole People. I explained that to Ms. Valliere. We are a civilized society that has chosen to live underground rather than in that crime-ridden cesspool of a city that lies above us. Some of the people down here even have jobs up above, and come below at the end of the day, just like anyone else who commutes to work. The night in the city above can be a very scary place, but down here, it's peaceful. But the Mole People," he looked down for a second, then glanced back up at Jack. "They are an entirely different breed. I explained that to Ms. Valliere, but I fear it only got her more interested."

"Then who are the Mole People?" Mike asked.

"This city we've built," the commissioner gestured toward one of the windows. "The entire city is constructed within an unused subway station, a terminal to be exact. A juncture for several new subway lines. It's fairly clean and we keep it that way. But the Mole People, they inhabit old sewer tunnels. Dark, fetid lines and junctures, long unused and forgotten by the city Sewer Department. They can hardly be called people. They were down here long before us, probably for generations. They've inbred to keep their race going. They never go up to the surface, content to wander the black tunnels. Though their eyes are large and round, devoid of pupils, we believe they've long lost their ability to see. They most likely find their way around with some type of sonar sense, like bats. Their skin is pale, never seeing the light of day. They feed on track rats and have shown cannibalistic tendencies. They can no longer be called human. They are an entirely different race and very dangerous. They mostly live like animals. Though recently, we've heard they've become more organized. They have a leader. We call him the Great King Rat. He seems larger, stronger and more intelligent than the rest."

"And you told Lavonne about them?" Jack asked, knowing she'd become very intrigued by that information. She was a curious gal. It's what made her such a great reporter.

"Yes, I'm afraid." He sighed. "I warned her about how dangerous they were, to stay away from their domain. Be happy with what she learned from staying with us."

"And she agreed?" Mike asked.

"She seemed to. The next morning, I got up to find she had gone. I assumed she had enough for her story and returned to her world."

"But she never came back up," Jack said, seething.

"It appears not. I fear for what might have become of her."

Jack tried not to think of the possibility of her beautiful figure ending up in the hands of those putrid creatures, to possibly be -- eaten.

"We have to go looking for her," Jack said, rising out of his chair, fists clenched, his blood boiling.

"It may already be too late," the commissioner said, looking up at him.

"We need to try," Mike said, also standing up. "And we shouldn't wait any longer."

"You'll need help," the commissioner said. "A guide."

"I can go," Max said.

"No," the commissioner put out his arm to halt him from rising. "Thank you Max, but we need you here. I have someone else in mind."

···

They walked down the middle of the causeway of Twilight City, and Jack was amazed as he took in the sights around him. It was just like a real community. There was a woman hanging laundry on a clothesline, kids playing jacks beside a small home, a man on a ladder putting a fresh coat of paint on the side of a building.

"How long have you been down here?" Jack asked Titus.

"Me? Gosh, it's been so long I lose track of time."

"How did you end up down here?" Mike asked.

"Well, I was a professor of sociology at a university in the city. I was on sabbatical and, like your intrepid reporter, had heard the rumors about a society beneath the city. I was skeptical of course. But I found my way down here and was amazed at what I had found. Of course, it wasn't quite as well organized as you see here," he waved his arm about. "But I helped them get more organized, all in the name of scientific research. Then it got to the point where I liked it better down here."

"Why?" Mike asked.

Titus stopped and turned to face them.

"My wife was raped and murdered up in the city one day." He paused, glancing down solemnly, and then looked up. "Lost my zest for life, became despondent. That's why I was on a sabbatical. Then I discovered this place and helped them build a society I preferred living in."

They continued walking until Titus stopped in front of a building.

The three of them entered the door-less entryway.

It was a library. Great tall bookcases reached to the ceiling, shelves stacked with books.

"Where'd you get all these books?" Jack asked, eyes scanning the stacks.

"You'd be surprised how much stuff people toss away in your world." He looked around. "Murphy?"

"Yes?" came a voice from deep within the building. They followed the sound down an aisle where a tall skinny man stood up on a ladder, shelving a handful of books.

"Alvin Murphy," Titus informed them as the man descended the ladder. "He's been residing down here a long time and knows these tunnels as well as anyone."

After a round of handshakes, the commissioner filled Murphy in on what was going on.

"I'd sure hate to think anything's happened to Miss Valliere," he said upon completion, slowly shaking his head.

"Will you help them?" Titus asked. "I know it's asking a lot."

"Of course," Murphy said, without hesitation.

"Even if you just take them as far as the Steam Pipe."

"No, they'll need my guidance well beyond that."

"The Steam Pipe?" Mike asked.

"It separates the subway lines from the sewer lines," Titus explained.

"Their world from ours," Murphy added.

"When can we go?" Jack asked.

"Immediately," he answered. "Just let's grab some supplies and we'll be off."

•••

The three of them walked at a quick pace down a long dimly lit corridor, their shoes clacking on the stone floor. They did not speak, just pushed forward toward their destination, each carrying an electric torch light. Murphy led the way with a satchel slung over his shoulder. Mike had been given back his service revolver and that was a little comforting to Jack considering what unknown dangers lay ahead. They also returned the knife to Jack, and he had it in his pocket, hoping though that he wouldn't have to use it. Jack studied Mike's face and could see something was on his mind. He watched Mike staring at Murphy as they walked along in silence.

"What's on your mind?" Jack whispered to Mike.

"This guy," Mike whispered back. "Something familiar about him."

Whether he heard them or not, Murphy did not let on.

Something clicked in Mike's thought waves.

"Alvin Murphy, I know that name."

"It's just a name," Murphy said.

"You were a war hero, in the Great War."

Murphy stopped and turned to Mike.

"I was no hero."

"Of course you were," Mike jabbed Jack in the arm. "You won the congressional Medal of Honor. I remember reading all about you."

"Is that true?" Jack asked.

"I did what I did for my brothers in arms. That's all." He turned away. "Nothing more."

"You manned a machine gun nest alone during an enemy assault." Mike was giddy with excitement, like a little kid. "You must have mowed down thirty or forty Germans. Saved your whole platoon."

"It's something I try to forget, though I doubt I ever will." He cast his eyes downward. "I was helping covering our unit's retreat, trying to buy them some time while they withdrew. The enemy kept coming, and I kept pouring fire on them. I wished they would stop, but they didn't. They were a stubborn enemy. They were getting ripped to shreds by my machine gun fire, but they wouldn't stop. They were like mindless animals, oblivious to the death and destruction of the lead raining upon them." Murphy shook his head vigorously. "It was horrible, but I had to keep it up, to protect my fellow soldiers. To me they were nothing but animals that had been hunting us and haunting us for months, trying to kill us. They were screaming as they charged forward into the gunfire, and I was screaming right back for them to stop. But they kept coming, through the smoke of the fire, 'til they were no more." He paused and took a deep breath. "When the smoke cleared and the sound of the machine gun's echoes died, I could hear the wounded moaning in pain. And even though I didn't understand the German language, I could hear some of them, and knew they were crying out for their mothers. That made me realize they weren't animals, they were human beings, just like me."

He stopped and neither Mike nor Jack knew how to respond. Mike seemed struck by the wonder of the tale, like some young kid listening to a radio show.

"How'd you end up down here?" Jack asked.

Murphy looked back at them. "I saw horrors beyond imagination over there. I saw what vile things men were capable of doing to one another." His gaze dropped to his feet. "When I came back, I decided this was not the kind of world I wanted to live in."

Jack and Mike were silent.

"I found my way down here, discovered this peaceful existence. I've never touched a weapon since. And never will." Murphy turned and walked away, and they followed.

At last they came to a large circular hole in the wall, about four feet off the ground.

"This is The Steam Pipe," Murphy said.

They peered in. Jack saw a long narrow tunnel with a faint light at the other end.

"This leads to the Dark Zone, where the Mole People live."

Jack and Mike glanced at each other.

"If Lavonne Valliere's gone through there, God help her soul."

"These Mole People pretty nasty, huh?" Mike asked.

"They're not the only dangers lurking in the Dark Zone."

"What else is there?" Jack asked.

"The Blizzard roams the sewer waters of the Dark Zone." He saw the curiosity on his companions' faces. "He's a large albino alligator. Been living down here for many years. Probably was someone's pet flushed down a toilet when it started to get too big."

"You've got to be kidding," Jack said.

"I've never seen it myself," Murphy said. "Only the body parts of its victims, so I don't doubt it's out there."

Jack stared into The Steam Pipe again. Did they really want to go in there? But, they had to. They had to find Lavonne.

"There's also the Black Devil."

"What's that?" Mike asked.

"A murderous psychopath who roams the tunnels wearing a dark hooded cloak. He carries a saber and can cut a man to shreds before the blink of an eye. He lives for the pure pleasure of killing."

"Oh geez," Jack said, glancing into the tunnel again. "Quite a circus of horrors you got down here. And you prefer this to the world up top?"

"If you stay out of the Dark Zone, you're okay. They usually don't stray to this side of The Steam Pipe."

"But into the mouth of madness we need to go," Jack said.

"After you," Mike replied.

"I'll go first," Murphy said. "We go one at a time, and no man starts till the other reaches the end."

"Why's that?" Jack asked.

Murphy tapped the side of the pipe. "This Steam Pipe is a conduit for the pressured steam generated beneath the city. There's a relief valve that lets loose when too much pressure builds up in the lines. The steam escapes through this pipe." He looked at the two of them. "And it's over a thousand degrees. It'll boil you in your shoes before you know it."

Jack shook his head.

"Nothing's easy down here."

"If you hear the pipes start to bang, you'll know you need to move your ass. Unless you want to be cooked like a lobster."

Murphy grabbed some rags from his satchel. "Here, wrap these around your hands to protect them from the hot metal." He stuck his light into the front of his pants and crawled into the pipe.

Jack and Mike stood by and watched Murphy wiggle his way down the long dark pipe. He scurried like a cat, or more appropriate down here, like a rat. He barely made a sound. Soon they heard his voice calling from the other end.

"Okay."

"You go next," Jack said to Mike.

He watched as Mike struggled to maneuver down the pipe, taking nearly twice as long as Murphy, and a heck of a lot more noisy. After what seemed an endless wait, Mike hollered from the other end.

Jack clambered up into the pipe and took a deep breath. He could feel heat on his knees through the cloth of his pants. He clenched his fists tight around the rags on his hands and worked his way down the pipe. It was stuffy, and he breathed in the thick air. It didn't seem like he was making much progress. The circular light at the other end looked very tiny, with the two small heads staring back at him. He attempted to crawl faster, slipped and banged his head.

Before long, the light at the other end finally began to appear bigger. He must be more than halfway, he thought. He didn't realize how out of shape he was. It was a struggle to keep moving. But he did. Just a little further he thought, before he might pass out.

Something banged. A low metallic sound.

"What was that," he called out.

"Pick up the pace, Jack," Murphy said his voice even-toned.

The banging grew louder and Jack squirmed through the pipe toward the other end.

"Come on Jack," Mike yelled, his voice frenetic. "Faster."

Jack tried, but it seemed the harder he tried to move quickly, the slower he took.

A hissing sound arose over his head.

"Get moving, Jack," Murphy yelled, no longer calm.

Jack could see them clearer, just up ahead. Heat began building in the pipe and sweat ran down Jack's brows into his eyes. A whooshing sound came from behind, but Jack didn't dare look over his shoulder. He didn't want to see the white cloud pushing toward him. He could feel it, though. His hands started burning through the rags, the heat wrapping around his body.

He could see Murphy and Mike, their hands reaching out toward him. Then a great hot wave pushed at him from behind, and he nearly collapsed. Hands grabbed his, and he was yanked forward, out of the pipe and spilling onto the cement floor. He heard something crack.

The three of them lay close to the ground as jets of steam poured out of the pipe over their heads and dissipated up into the ceiling.

It stopped as quickly as it started. Jack looked at the others.

"I'm all right?" he asked, barely able to catch his breath.

Murphy shined a torch on him.

"Just a little pink," he said.

Jack looked down at his normally pale hands and saw they were a little flushed.

"I never could tan," he said. "That's why I don't go to the beach." He also saw that his light had broken in the fall. He shook it a few times, realized it was hopeless and tossed it away. At least the others had lights.

They stood up and Murphy shined his light around the large vestibule they were in. Jack sensed right away the heavy putrid odor on this side of the steam pipe.

"Is it wise to use a light?" Mike asked. "Won't it help them see us?"

"We don't have the advantage of their abilities in the dark," Murphy said. "Besides, I have no doubt they already know we're here."

He signaled with the light. "This way."

Jack and Mike followed.

An arched doorway led out of the vestibule to a small brick-lined tunnel. A fetid odor rose from the water flowing down the middle of the tunnel.

"This is where we get our feet wet," Murphy said, leading the way.

They barely had enough room to stand erect as they waded into the calf-high water.

"God, this stinks!" Jack said, grimacing. He couldn't believe Lavonne would come down this way, but then by this point in her journey, she could have been taken by force, not choice. If she was even still alive.

As the torch light brushed against the brick walls around them, Jack could see cockroaches scurrying along the walls. Big ones too. Some almost the size of a fist. Every few steps, one would drop from the ceiling onto his shoulder and he'd brush it off with a shiver. His feet were cold as the water seeped into his shoes and socks.

Jack could see something floating in the water up ahead in the light of the torch.

"What's that?" Jack said, pointing. He immediately thought of The Blizzard, but this object didn't seem that large. As they got closer, they could see it was a body.

Oh no, Jack thought. Not Lavonne, please not Lavonne.

When they came upon it, they could tell it was a man's body, floating. Murphy pulled it out of the water a bit and Jack saw it had no head.

"Oh god," Mike exclaimed.

Jack had seen a lot of crime victims in his career as a reporter. He had witnessed his share of stabbings and shootings. But this was the first time seeing a decapitation.

"What did that?" Jack said.

"Was it that alligator, you think?" Mike asked. "The Great Blizzard."

"No," Murphy said, letting the body drop back into the water and pushing it away, to float off behind them. "The cut was too clean on the neck. Besides, the Great Blizzard wouldn't have left that much behind. That looks more like the work of the Black Devil."

They continued on, Jack glancing behind as the headless body floated away into the darkness. He shivered.

Up ahead, Murphy stopped. The tunnel forked into two separate passageways.

"Which way?" Jack asked.

"Take your pick," Murphy replied.

"Wait a minute," Mike said, stepping over to the right-hand tunnel entrance. "Look at this." He pointed to the wall. There was a red V on it.

"Oh my god," Jack said. "Did Lavonne mark that?" Was she leaving a trail?

"It looks like lipstick," Mike said. He brought his face close to the wall and kissed the V. "Yep, I recognize that lipstick. It's Lavonne's."

Jack was stunned. He's kissed her, he thought. He couldn't believe it. Why would she have kissed him? He knew Mike liked her, but had they ever dated? He felt a twinge of jealousy.

They stood before the V on the wall of the right hand tunnel. "Then that's the way we'll go," Murphy said, plunging ahead.

Jack followed behind Mike, still bothered by the whole lipstick scene. He was now thinking it might not have been a good idea bringing Mike with him. If they managed to rescue her, Mike would get to share in the heroism. And if Lavonne had been out with Mike, she would certainly find it very chivalrous. Jack wanted the glory of saving her all his own. Maybe then she would see him more than just a co-worker and friend. Maybe something a lot more.

The tunnel broadened as they proceeded; the water subsided to a trickle. Another tunnel branched off to the right. There was another red V, so they continued down that way.

How much deeper underground were they going, Jack wondered. How much deeper under the city?

Murphy stopped suddenly. Jack almost bumped into Mike as he stopped as well. There was a scratching sound ahead.

"Quiet," Murphy whispered.

Jack listened. It sounded like something ahead scratching on the bricks.

"What is it?" Jack asked.

"I don't know," Murphy said, shining his light deeper into the tunnel. There was only darkness. "Move slowly."

They proceeded at a brief pace, Jack searching the dimly lit way. He could almost picture Lavonne crawling along the tunnel, her once beautiful painted nails scratching the bricks as she dragged herself along, trying to escape the horrors that had befallen her.

The scratching seemed to be joined by more. Mike removed his gun. Jack felt his pocket where he had put the knife, just to make sure it was still there. Murphy stabbed the beam of light ahead and it caught a pair of red glowing eyes. Jack froze, nobody moved. Was it one of the Mole People, Jack thought? There were more pairs of eyes and as the light focused, Jack saw they were rats. But these were like no rats Jack had ever seen. They had to be the size of large dogs. Their snouts were long and crooked and the jaws opened to reveal sharp teeth and a drooling tongue. There were almost a dozen of them.

"Don't move," Murphy said.

Mike kept his gun trained ahead.

"They're probably more afraid of us then we are of them."

"I doubt that," Jack said, his heart pounding in his chest, his feet frozen to the ground.

"Maybe we can scare them off," Mike said softly, waving his gun.

Jack looked up at the ceiling and saw a rat clinging to the bricks, hanging upside down. Bat wings spread out from its back, and it released its grip.

"Watch out!" Jack yelled as the rat flew toward them.

Mike fired at it, missing. The other rats scrambled toward them.

"Go back!" Murphy screamed, pushing Jack.

Jack ran, not daring to look back, but hearing the footsteps of the others behind him and the clattering of claws on the bricks. Another shot echoed in the tunnel. Jack kept running, saw the branch they had passed and turned into it, running blind into the darkness. He kept his hands out in front of him, expecting to run into a stone wall. He realized he could not hear the others following him and stopped. What happened to them? Had the rats got them? No. He would have heard their screams, because no doubt, based on their size and the crazed looks on those horrid faces there would have been screaming. Jack kept moving through the darkness, slowly not liking how he couldn't see where he was going. Was he going toward them, or further away from them. He called out. Nothing. *Dammit,* he thought. *How the hell did I manage to get separated from them?* And they had the lights.

Jack kept moving, knowing the rats could still be nearby, but he wouldn't be able to see them. Every slight sound in the tunnel caused his head to jerk around. He kept his right hand outstretched, touching the rough wall, feeling his way along. His hand touched something and whatever it was, it moved. A cockroach? Maybe. He put his hand on the wall and continued.

Suddenly, he took a step and felt nothing beneath his foot. His body pitched forward, and he felt himself falling. *Oh god,* he thought, plunging down into darkness. He hit water and became submerged, touched bottom and propelled himself back up.

He was waist deep in filthy mucky fetid water. It made him gag and he vomited. Hacking and coughing, he wiped his sleeve across his mouth. He looked around but could not see anything. With his arms outstretched he tried to feel his way.

"Hello!" He yelled. "Mike! Alvin! Can you hear me?"

He thought he heard a faint response from far away. He moved in that direction, slowly through the water. Sound was hard to pinpoint down here, he had noticed, and he worried he could be moving further and further away from them. He could get lost down here and they would never find him. Wouldn't Swanson have a fit losing two reporters? Jack snickered.

There was a splash behind him and Jack spun around.

Was something in the water with him? Was it the Blizzard? God, how he wanted to get out of this cold, stinky, disgusting water. That thing could be under the water right now, circling him. Do alligators circle? He knew sharks did. No, he doubted it. Alligators seemed like they would just launch straight at you. He tried to see the dark surface of the water, see if there was any rippling of something moving just beneath the surface. But it was so dark, he couldn't tell where the water ended and the wall began.

Jack took a few steps backward. God, he wished he could see. He stopped.

Something sharp pressed against the side of his neck, and he froze.

"Don't move," a deep voice whispered as a hand reached around his chest. The blade pressed closer into his skin.

"I won't," Jack said, trembling, suspecting immediately he was in the clutches of the Black Devil. He thought about the headless corpse he had seen as he felt the cold steel on his neck. His Adam's apple bobbed up and down in his throat as he tried to swallow, but his mouth was too dry with fear.

"What are you doing here?" the voice whispered.

"I - I- I'm just looking for someone." He could barely get the words out.

"There's no one down here for you."

"Then, I'll just leave if that's okay with you."

"No," the voice whispered. "You'll never leave here." The blade pressed harder.

A swath of light pounced on them and Jack felt himself spun around.

"Let him go!" Murphy yelled, shining the light on them. Mike stood beside him, pointing his pistol at the Black Devil.

The cloaked figure held Jack tight, drawing the blade up to his throat.

"I'll cut his head off," he said, his voice no longer a whisper.

"I'll drop you before you get the chance," Mike said.

Shoot him, Jack thought. Shoot the bastard.

For the moment, nobody dared to make a move. Jack could feel the blade against his throat. Somebody do something, he thought, because he didn't trust that this maniac wouldn't draw that steel through his jugular. He could feel the blood pulsing through that artery and knew the slightest nick would send his life fluids spraying out his neck like a fire hose.

A great splash of water erupted behind them and Jack felt the grip on him release. There was a giant roar and Jack spun around to see the albino alligator rise from the water, its jaws opening.

"Jesus," Jack said, scrambling backwards through the water. The thing was huge, its large mouth filled with enormous pointed teeth. The Black Devil stood his ground, dwarfed before the large beast, his dark cloak flowing behind him from the wind of the monster's roar.

The Blizzard lunged forward at the Black Devil who thrust his saber into the gaping mouth. The jaws clamped down and the Black Devil screamed. A jerk of its neck and the Blizzard ripped the arm off. The man stood still, staring down at his missing arm and the blood spurting from the jagged stump. The Black Devil let out an ear-piercing bellow that echoed throughout the walls of the chamber. Jack wondered if the psychopath was more upset at losing his arm, or losing his sword.

Jack watched in horror as the alligator's jaws opened wide once more. Jack could see the blood dripping from its pointed teeth. The gator sprung forward, jaws snapping shut around the Black Devil's midsection. He writhed and screamed, struggling in the alligator's deadly grip, pounding its snout with his only remaining fist.

Jack felt someone grab his shoulder.

"Let's get out of here while we can," Murphy said.

They quickly scrambled through the water, leaving the screams echoing behind them. After a while the screams died out, and Jack figured the Black Devil was fully in the belly of the beast. He had no sympathy for the man. A minute ago, the killer would have gladly sliced his head off with that sword. So, as gruesome a way that was for any man to go, he did not care. The fiend got what he deserved. The Black Devil most likely didn't have any sympathy for all his victims. So Jack wasn't about to go shedding any tears. But still, he couldn't imagine anything more horrible, and he had already seen quite a few horrors down here. He wondered how many more lay in wait ahead.

Jack looked at Murphy ahead of him, determined as he led the way, as if the scene they had just left behind them had never happened. *He's probably seen a lot down here, and over in Europe before this.* Nothing seemed to bother him.

Mike was a different story. Even in the dim light, he could see Mike's face, pale and shaken. Jack didn't like that. He needed Mike to be strong. For all of them. And especially for Lavonne.

•••

The thing was huge, its large mouth filled with enormous pointed teeth.

Exhausted, Jack and the others trudged slowly through the water till they came to a spot where a slight ledge ran along the tunnel wall. With what energy he could muster Jack climbed up onto the ledge. At least now they could keep out of the water.

They rested for a few minutes in silence, turning their lights off to conserve the batteries. Jack noticed how much he was getting used to seeing in the dark. It wasn't as black as before, now that his eyes were adjusting to the world down here. Jack thought of Lavonne being down here and going through some of the same things they've been experiencing. She was beautiful, but strong, that's what most men loved about her. Hell, that's what Jack loved about her, and he was sure that's the way Mike felt. Yet, as tough a gal as she thought she was, how the hell could she endure this madness down here?

They walked on in silence, too tired and too frightened by their experiences to converse. They just plodded forward, Jack was not even certain Murphy knew where he was leading them, only that it was deeper into the tunnels.

The sound of the sewer water dissipated behind them, as it veered off along another route. Murphy stopped and shut off his light.

"What's going on?" Jack whispered.

"Quiet. There's something ahead," Murphy said softly. "Some kind of movement." He motioned them to get down and they crawled forward on their bellies, and then signaled them to stop. Jack lay still, not daring to move, barely daring to breathe. He could hear a shuffling up ahead, and then saw shadows moving. It was three figures, hunched over, moving along the tunnel. Jack knew it was them: The Mole People. He felt his heart race. He reached down and felt the knife in his pocket, reassuring himself it was still there.

Murphy tapped him on the shoulder, put a finger to his lips and motioned to move forward. They crept ahead, keeping low and heading in the direction the figures had departed. Jack sensed they were getting close. But close to what, he had no idea.

They moved on in silence and in the dark. But they could see where they were going.

Up ahead a faint glow emanated through an archway. They crept toward it and passed under the arch. They were in a cavernous room, the ceiling rising fifty feet above them. Torches lined masonry walls and there was movement below.

The three of them crawled to the lip of a ledge and peered over it.

A dark throng moved below, like a mass of insects. There must have been a hundred figures in dark rags huddled on the cavern floor. The torches cast streaks of light that caught the figures, and Jack saw pale skinless misshapen heads with bulging pupil-less eyes. A deep guttural growling rumbled among the mass below that echoed throughout the cavern. A putrid stench rose from the creatures up toward the ledge Jack peered over. There they were, the Mole People. They gathered around a circular opening in the floor, about twenty feet in diameter. A tall pillar stood beside the opening. Tied to it was Lavonne Valliere.

"There she is," Jack exclaimed, almost too loud.

Alvin clamped his hand over Jack's mouth and motioned him to keep quiet.

"Sorry," Jack whispered, his heart thudding rapidly in his chest at the excitement that Lavonne was still alive. He resisted the urge to race down there to save her.

She looked tattered, her shirt torn revealing pale flesh and a black brassiere, her pants were grimy. Her arms were clasped over her head, bound to the pillar by ropes. She struggled against the bindings, a frantic look on her face.

Jack ached, wanting to call out to her, tell her they were on their way to save her. God, they were so close, but they still had a huge obstacle to overcome. They couldn't just march down there in the middle of that horde of mutants. That would be suicidal madness. They needed to come up with some kind of plan.

"Look there," Murphy pointed.

Above the cavern floor, behind the pillar, jutted out a stone terrace. A tall broad figure strode to the edge of the terrace overlooking the cavern floor. He was dressed in a dark cape and wore a colorful tribal mask over his face.

"The Great King Rat," Murphy whispered.

The figure raised his arms above his head. The growling from the Mole People decreased in volume until it settled to a slight murmur.

"Great and obedient followers," The Great King Rat said in a booming voice that echoed throughout the cavern.

Jack looked at the others in surprise. Whoever the Great King Rat was, he was certainly not like the rest of these monsters. No, he was human.

"An intruder has dared to enter our domain. This is not allowed!"

The crowd roared an almost ape-like growl.

"We are the dwellers of the tunnels," the figure exclaimed. "I, your master, will lead you against the outsiders and we will rule the underworld."

More howls came from the Mole People as they bobbed up and down in excitement.

"No one will stand in our way. We will put out their lights and feast upon the darkness."

Jack was amazed at how enthralled and mesmerized this man's minions behaved before their leader. It showed that they weren't quite the mindless monsters he thought they were.

"He reminds me of the mayor," Mike chuckled, and Jack couldn't help crack a smile that seemed to relieve the tension ever so slightly.

"But first," the Great King Rat bellowed, "we must appease our god!"

Jack wondered what kind of god these monsters would worship.

"So, we gather here to offer this sacrifice to our worthy god!"

The Mole People moaned and swayed to his words.

"Sacrifice," Mike said. "I don't like the sound of that."

"We better move quickly," Murphy said.

Jack looked around them and saw steps leading from either side of the ledge they were on.

"So what's the plan?" he asked.

Murphy scanned the scene while the Great King Rat prattled to his followers below, his voice echoing off the cavern walls.

"You two go down the right," he said pointing. "Get to Lavonne. I'll take the left here and go after the big rat."

"And then?" Mike asked.

"I don't know," he shrugged. "I'm making this up as we go along."

Mike withdrew his gun and held it ready. Murphy put his hand on Mike's shoulder.

"Be careful with that," he whispered, pointing up toward the cavern ceiling. Jack could see pipes running along the walls high up. "Gas pipes," Murphy said. "Don't know if they're active, but one stray bullet and …"

"Kaboom," Mike finished, nodding.

Murphy handed Jack his light and headed off to the stairs on the left.

Jack and Mike crept softly down the stone steps along the right side of the cavern. Jack held the knife in his hand, with the blade open. He could see Murphy scampering along the left side. Lavonne writhed against her restraints, trying her best to get free while the throng of Mole People wavered in front. Jack couldn't take his eyes off the dark hole in front of the pillar. What would the sacrifice be, he wondered? Throw her down that dark pit? What was down there?

They reached the bottom of the cavern floor undetected. The Mole People's attention was captivated by Lavonne and The Great King Rat, so no one noticed them. Jack could see Murphy was edging closer to the terrace.

"Come forth oh god and feast upon our sacrifice!" The Great King Rat bellowed, as the Mole People formed a ring around the dark pit.

There was a loud clattering sound, and Jack realized it was coming from the pit. His eyes widened with horror as two large antennas appeared out of the hole, followed by the head of a giant cockroach. Its front legs gripped the edge of the pit and pulled itself up.

Lavonne screamed.

"Jesus!" Mike cried. Jack was stunned into silence. It looked the size of a bus.

Mike rushed forward, pushing through the crowd of Mole People, shoving them aside and firing his pistol at the head of the beast. Jack unfroze and quickly followed. Sharp-clawed arms grabbed at him as he ran by, tearing at his clothes and his flesh.

"Stop!" The Great King Rat yelled. "Stop the intruders!" He reached beneath his cape and withdrew a Tommy gun, aiming down into the cavern and releasing a burst of machine gun fire.

The bullets danced around Jack, hitting mostly the Mole People who were trying to grab him, sending blood and bits of pale flesh flying in all directions. Jack felt something wet hit the side of his face, but brushed it off without stopping, or looking to see what it was.

Mike managed to get between the Lavonne and the giant cockroach, emptying his gun into its head. His chambers empty, he quickly reached into his pocket for more bullets.

Jack saw the head of the beast bend down.

"Watch out, Mike!" Jack yelled.

The cockroach's jaws quickly reached forward and clamped around Mike's waist, lifting him up into the air. He screamed, pounding his fists helplessly upon the beast, his eyes wide with terror.

"NO!" Jack screamed.

The insect bit down and a gusher of blood shot out from Mike's body as he wailed in excruciating agony. Jack reached Lavonne as bullets still rained down around him from above.

"Jack!" Lavonne said, with a weak voice. "Oh Jack!" She seemed surprised and relieved to see him. "I was praying you would make it here in time."

Jack looked up in horror at the sound of crunching bones as the cockroach swallowed the body of Mike Emerson, his screams ceasing.

"Oh God," Lavonne exclaimed, exhaling an exasperated breath. "Poor Mike. How awful."

"Yeah," Jack frantically cut the rope restraints holding Lavonne to the pillar. "And we're next on the menu if we don't hurry." He glanced up in time to see Murphy leaping onto the back of The Great King Rat.

As Jack released the restraints, Lavonne collapsed onto his shoulder, exhausted. Jack looked back and saw the cockroach moving toward them. He looked frantically around. There was nowhere to go. They were trapped. He pushed Lavonne behind him and held the knife out in front of him, a seemingly useless weapon against such a behemoth.

A burst of gunfire pelted the cockroach's head, green guts spurting out, and Jack looked up to see Murphy, with the Tommy gun in hand, firing at the creature.

"Get out of there, Jack!" he yelled.

Jack grabbed Lavonne's hand and pulled her along, slugging a few of the Mole People that got in his way with the knife in his closed fist. The knife cut through the soft mushy flesh of the creatures like pudding. He could feel the bones in their faces cracking and collapsing from the force of his fists. He glanced behind him to see the dying insect slip back down the pit.

He practically had to drag Lavonne up the steps to the terrace, she was so weak. The Mole People followed close behind. Up on the terrace Jack saw Murphy blasting away at the Mole People with the Tommy gun. The gun emptied and he grabbed another drum magazine that was lying at his feet.

"Where's the rat?" Jack asked.

"He escaped down that passage behind me," Murphy screamed over the echoing of the gun blasts. "Maybe it's a way out."

Jack and Lavonne headed to the passage. He looked back at Murphy.

"You coming?"

"I'll keep holding them off. You two get going." He slammed the magazine into the gun.

Jack hurriedly led Lavonne down the passage, listening to the machine gun fire behind him, hoping Murphy would be all right.

At the end of the passage they came to a metal gate. Jack opened it and was faced with three blank walls.

"A dead end?" Lavonne said.

"No," Jack said, hearing gears grinding. He shone his light upwards. "It's an elevator shaft."

•••

"What do we do now?" Lavonne asked.

Jack scanned his torch light around the shaft. The framework of the shaft was made from thick 2-by-6's, spaced horizontally about six feet apart.

He looked at Lavonne. "We climb."

Jack let Lavonne go first so he could keep an eye on her if she struggled. He stuffed the torch into the front of his pants so its light could shine the trek above them. Behind him, the bursts of machine gun fire continued, and he wondered how Murphy was holding out.

The climb was hard, and Jack worried about Lavonne's strength, knowing how sapped his own was. He wondered how high the shaft went. It had already seemed liked they had climbed a great deal, but it didn't feel like they had gotten anywhere. Above was dark and quiet.

They continued in silence, the exertion filling his lungs with tremendous pressure, leaving little room for breathing, let alone talking.

Down below an explosion roared that shook the shaft.

"Hang on!" Jack yelled. He looked down and saw a ball of flame rising toward him. One of Murphy's bullets must have struck a gas pipe. "It's gonna get hot baby!"

Jack buried his face against the wall, gripping the wood beam. He felt a great wave of heat licking the soles of his feet. Then the heat dissipated as quickly as it came and he dared to look down and saw the flames receding down the shaft. Jack's shoes were smoking. He wondered if Murphy was all right.

Jack looked up at Lavonne, glad to see her still hanging on above him.

"Okay, keep moving."

Lavonne glanced down at him and he could see exhaustion in her eyes as she grimaced. Then she looked up and proceeded to grab onto the next beam and pull herself up.

At one point, Lavonne stopped, clinging to the wood beam but not moving. "Jack," she said, between exhausted breaths. "I don't know if I can go on."

"We have no choice," he said, looking down at the smoky bottom of the shaft. "There's no going down anymore." H reached up and planted his right palm under the soft curve of her buttocks and pushed. "Keep going."

They continued. Reach up, pull up, step up. On and on, upwards. Lavonne didn't say another word to him, saving her strength for the climb instead.

From above came a loud bang followed by a metallic scraping and whooshing sound.

"Stop!" Jack yelled.

"What is it?" Lavonne asked.

Jack could hear a rattling sound getting louder and realized the elevator was coming down toward them, and coming down fast. The Great King Rat must have cut the cable.

"It's the elevator!" he screamed.

Jack scrambled up to the level with Lavonne and pressed her into the wall of the shaft, pressing his body into hers, trying to squeeze their bodies into the nook between the two-by-sixes. He braced himself, holding tight, hoping there was enough room.

"Hang on!" he yelled into her ear.

The elevator car sounded like a locomotive as it barrelled down on them, pushing air ahead of it like a hot steaming breath. The sound was deafening and Jack held his breath. At its loudest Jack felt something hard scrape along his back, tearing his shirt. Then it was past, hurtling to the bottom. Jack was knocked off balance and felt he was going to fall backwards, worried he'd drag Lavonne down with him. He regained his hold and kept still, hearing a loud crash from the bottom of the shaft.

"You okay?" he whispered into Lavonne's ear, which was an inch from his lips.

"Yes," she said with a heavy breath. "You?"

"I'm all right, I think." But he felt a wet sensation trickling down his back and knew it was blood. "That was close. Let's continue."

He wasn't sure what waited for them above. They could be just climbing their way to their own deaths. But there was no other choice now. Down was not an option.

Jack looked up above at a rectangular shape that was not as black as the rest of the shaft.

He switched off the torch. It must be the elevator opening.

They finally reached it, and he pushed Lavonne up into it. Then he reached up to the edge, grabbing hold of thick shag carpet and pulled. He didn't think he had enough strength to get himself up, hanging there feeling like he'd come so far, but couldn't make this last obstacle. He thought his arms would give out, pitching his body down into the darkness below.

But then he felt Lavonne grab hold of his arms, and he kicked his legs as she helped pull him onto the floor. They rolled over onto their backs on the carpet, exhausted, panting heavily, just wanting to rest. The softness of the rug was soothing and he felt he could easily pass out.

Jack sat up abruptly. There was still danger. He looked around, trying to see where he was. It was a large room with a big desk over by one wall. Out the windows to his left he could see the city lights. They were quite a few stories up.

His eyes focused as he stood. The wall behind the desk held an African tribal shield.

"Oh my god," he said to Lavonne, who now stood beside him. "This is Harrison Swanson's office." He noticed a space on the wall where one of the tribal masks had hung. Also, the spear was missing.

"Exactly," a voice boomed to their right.

They turned and there was Swanson, dressed in his cape, holding the spear in his hand. On the floor at his feet lay the tribal mask he had been wearing in the cavern.

"The Great King Rat," Jack said. "How fitting."

Swanson's face was red with rage, a vein throbbing on his forehead.

"I tried to warn you both not to go looking for the Mole People. But you didn't listen." He took a step forward, spear outthrust. "You picked the wrong time to be ace reporters. Now you've missed your last deadline."

Jack pushed Lavonne behind him.

"You're an insane megalomaniac," Jack said, keeping his eye on the sharp tip of the spear.

"No, not insane," Swanson said. "A king. I ruled over a whole kingdom down there, an empire. I stumbled upon them when I was a young reporter, much like yourselves. I became fascinated with them. And as I rose to the head of this paper, I realized I wanted to rule more than the news world. I wanted to rule a kingdom!"

"Your kingdom is gone."

"And so will you two be."

He lunged forward with the spear, his large eyes wild with madness. Jack tried to dodge the thrust, but the tip grazed his forearm, drawing a line of blood. Stinging pain ran up his arm. He pushed Lavonne further behind him, keeping himself between her and the madman.

Swanson grinned, a mad, wild grimace.

He swung the shaft at Jack's head; Jack ducked, almost losing his balance.

Swanson thrust the spear at him again.

Jack grabbed the shaft of the spear and swung Swanson around. The man was strong, and the two were in a tug-of-war with the spear, Swanson pushing the tip to within inches of Jack's chest. Jack didn't have much strength left after all he'd endured during his journey over the past few hours. He was drained and felt he could drop at any second. And then he would be at the mercy of the Great King Rat.

Jack hung onto the shaft as Swanson tried to pull it loose. Jack had to muster what remaining strength he could find deep within him. He gripped the shaft tight and pushed Swanson toward the elevator shaft.

"I didn't come all this way," Jack said through gritted teeth, "crawling through the corridors of that nightmarish hell down there, for it to end here."

Jack shoved the spear again.

Swanson's shoes caught the edge of the shaft opening and he stumbled. Jack pushed backwards and Swanson's eyes now bulged with fear as he held tight to the shaft of the spear, suddenly realizing it was the only thing preventing him from falling backwards.

Jack let go of the spear.

A long screamed followed as Swanson's body dropped into the shaft.

Jack and Lavonne crept close to the edge and peered down. She held her arm around his waist. Though they could see nothing, they heard the scream become fainter, 'til it was abruptly cut off.

"He's gone," Lavonne said, gripping Jack tighter.

Jack stared into the darkness, feeling the warmth of Lavonne's body close to him. "End of story."

THE END

The Idea For This Tale

In the 1980s I spent several years living in New York City. At the time, I remember hearing and reading about abandoned tunnels and subway stations beneath the city and how many of them were inhabited by homeless people. I had even read about a New York City journalist who had gained access to the tunnel people and was writing a book about the subject.

As a writer of horror tales, the idea of people living in a world beneath the city was fascinating. I filed the information away, hoping and knowing that eventually I would find some way of using it in a story. Though it inspired me, I purposely decided not to read the book the journalist eventually wrote about the tunnel people, because I didn't want it to influence my imagining of this extremely unusual world.

Fast forward a couple decades later and the story of the tunnel world still haunted me. Having recently written a pulp story for Airship 27, I thought the pulp era was a perfect setting for a story about the tunnel people.

This story spent so many years gelling in my imagination, that I don't quite remember how it all came together. I know I wanted to inhabit my tunnel world with all sorts of horrible things. Remember, I'm a horror writer by nature. So of course rats and cockroaches would play a part, and everyone has heard of the urban legend of the alligator that gets flushed down a toilet as a baby and grows large in the city sewers. So those things would all have to play a part in this world beneath the city.

I wanted the story to be visual and fast paced, like watching one of those old cliff-hanger serials from the '30s and '40s. Action and danger had to lurk around every corner, not to mention horror. And I had the opportunity to fill this world with an endless supply of hazards. The only limit was my imagination. Of course, like those old-time serials, I needed to have an action hero.

I spend almost two decades at a small town newspaper working side by side with news reporters. The character of crime reporter Jack Minch is based on a reporter I worked with. Though the Jack Minch in the story is a much exaggerated character than his real life counterpart, I could easily imagine the real Jack acting the same way in these circumstances. He wouldn't hesitate to go down into a mysterious tunnel to help a fellow reporter in distress. And he wouldn't let his editor stop him.

So now I created this pulp hero, ace crime reporter Jack Minch, and sent him down into the tunnel world. What would happen to him once he went down there, I wasn't quite sure. I had several scenes in mind, ones that I conjured up over those many years that this story lay dormant in my imagination. All I had to do was put the gears in motion and let it go. The beauty of writing is often I don't feel like I'm in control at all. There's something magical once the fingers start clicking on the keyboard and words flow from some deep recess of my imagination, as if someone, or something, else is writing the story and I'm just the conduit.

The story was ready to tell itself. Jack Minch was the key. How he reacted and responded in this unique world would be the key to telling this tale. Once Jack got moving, the story seemed to flow like the sewer waters in those tunnels seeking its way to the utter depths of the endless darkness below.

●●●

GREGORY BASTIANELLI - graduated from the University of New Hampshire where he studied fiction writing under authors Thomas Williams and Mark Smith. His stories have appeared in the print magazines *Black Ink Horror, Sinister Tales* and *Beyond Centauri*, the online magazines *Down in the Cellar* and *Absent Willow Review*, as well as the magazine anthologies *Encounters* and *Cover of Darkness*. His pulp story "The Dungeon of Death" appeared in Vol. I of Airship 27 Production's *Dan Fowler G-Man*. His debut horror novel, *Joker's Club*, will be released in November by JournalStone publishing. He lives in New Hampshire and can be reached at gregorybastianelli@yahoo.com

DOCK DOYLE

"Dock Doyle & the Wandering City"
By Adam Lance Garcia

Dock Doyle charged into the chamber, pistol drawn. Lightning flashed and thunder roared, reverberating through the stone tower. A warbling laughter echoed around him, nasal and venomous. "Do you really think you can stop me, Doyle? Do you really believe anyone can stop Doctor Dread?"

Dock pulled back the hammer of his pistol, eyeing the shadows. His heart pounded in his chest, beads of sweat poured down his brow. Somewhere in the darkness a lever was pulled and the Death Ray came to life, its immense, deadly engine glowing and whirring with menace. It was worse than he had feared. There was little time left. Dock aimed his pistol at the Death Ray's mechanisms when Doctor Dread appeared from behind the machine, howling with laughter as he dragged out Gloria Reinhardt, a blade pressed to her milk-white throat. "Want to destroy my machine, Doyle? Do you want to save Freedom City so badly?"

Doyle scowled and aimed his gun at Doctor Dread.

"Come any closer Doyle and I will gut her!" Dread screamed with maniacal delight, pressing the blade's edge against Gloria's throat, drawing a thin line of scarlet.

"Don't worry about me, Dock!" Gloria cried, her face stern despite the tears streaming down her cheeks. "Stop Dread before he destroys the city!"

"Yes!" Dread screeched. "Choose! Choose between your two loves! The woman or the city! Which will it be, Dock Doyle?! *Which will it be*?!"

His powerful blue eyes darting between the masked villain, the screaming woman and the massive instrument of death, Dock Doyle scoffed. A cynical smile curled the corners of his lips. Running his hand over his short black hair, he holstered his gun and turned to William Witney.

"You're kiddin' me."

Witney chewed the inside of his cheek as he shifted uncomfortably in his director's chair, curling the script in his hands into a narrow tube. Leaning forward, anger dripping off every word, he whispered: "Your line is 'How about *both*, Dread.'"

"I *know* what my line is, Witney," Doyle shot back. He pointed a thumb at Doctor Dread. "What I'm *saying* is *this* is a bunch of crap. It doesn't make any sense."

Witney's face tensed up, his eyes threatening to pop out of his skull as his upper lip twitched. "It 'doesn't make any sense?' Which part 'doesn't make any *sense*?!'" he hissed through gritted teeth.

"Where do you want me to begin?"

"It's a goddamn *serial*, Doyle. This is the way it goes; madman, damsel in distress, death ray, cliffhanger, come back next week. We're not tryin' to reinvent the *goddamn wheel* here."

"Willy?" Dread asked from the other side of set, removing his mask to reveal the frustrated visage of actor Harry Worth. "What's going on, Willy? We're losing the moment and I can't keep talking like this for too much longer, my throat's *killin'* me!"

"One *goddamn* second, Harry!" Witney growled before aiming his anger back at Dock. "Listen, Doyle, you signed a pretty nice deal with the studio, so put aside logic and follow the *goddamn* script!"

Doyle pressed his tongue against his cheek and let out a sharp, derisive laugh. "No."

His face red, Witney screamed: "Cut!" A loud siren sounded as he jumped out of his director's chair and stormed out into the darkened studio. "Gardner! Jimmy Gardner! Where are you, you weasel?"

•••

A tall, thin man stood at the craft table, cigarette rolling between his fingers. He wore a smile like his jacket, loose and easy, his teeth shining as he leaned over the script girl. "Seriously, sweetheart," he breathed, inching closer, his eyes roving over her petite frame. "I've got the names of every major director this side of the tar pits. I know every exec in the Little Three by their first name, and play golf with the execs over at the Big Five. You just say the word and I'll make you the next Ginger Rogers."

The script girl blushed and softly swatted the man's arm, choosing not to notice the wedding band on his left hand. "Oh, Mr. Gardner, you do go on!"

"Oh, yes…" Gardner chuckled wickedly. "Yes, I do."

"Gardner!" Witney shouted.

Gardner sighed as his smile collapsed. "Duty calls." He took a long drag of his cigarette and turned to the steaming director. "Mr. Witney. What can I do for you?"

"I need you to *talk* to your client," Witney growled, jabbing a finger into Gardner's narrow frame.

Gardner scrunched his forehead, looking at the director as if the man had suddenly sprouted a second head. "Dock Doyle isn't my *client*, Mr. Witney. He's America's Favorite Son," he replied, flicking away his cigarette. "I'm just the man who makes sure that everyone remembers it."

Witney sucked his teeth. "Fine. Tell 'America's Favorite Son' that he needs to follow the script."

Gardner placed a hand on the director's shoulder. "Need I remind you that Dock is not only the *star* of this serial, he is also the Executive Producer? If he doesn't follow the script that means we need a re-write." Gardner smiled at the script girl. "Sweetheart, could you give me a copy of the screenplay? We need to have a production meeting."

•••

Dock unconsciously massaged the old bullet wound in his left thigh, barely feeling the low, radiating pain that echoed out into his bones. "It doesn't make sense is the problem," he grumbled. "That doesn't happen in real life. No one goes around dressing like it's Halloween and tries to destroy a city."

"There's a man in Germany who might disagree with you on that point, Dock," Gardner said from the make-up chair, sipping a glass of scotch.

"You start reading the paper, Jimmy?"

Gardner shrugged. "I took in a newsreel or two."

"Be that as it may," Dock said, eyeing his agent with contempt, "The *Führer* doesn't wear a *mask*."

"But, Mr. Doyle, sir…" the screenwriter Nathaniel Wharton hesitantly began, nervously twirling a pencil between his fingers. "*That's* what happens in *your* pulps."

Dock glared at the young redhead. "And?"

Nathaniel cleared his throat and picked up a rolled up copy of *Dock Doyle Adventures #49* and thumbed to the beginning of "The Dreadful Machine" by Kenneth Robeson. Curling the cover back, Nathaniel showed Dock a black-and-white illustration of Dock grappling a masked Doctor Dread as they plummeted from a burning dirigible.

"Look, see? Right here," he said, pointing to the illustration. "That's *you* fighting Doctor Dread. The caption even reads: '*Dock Doyle* heard the explosion rip through the airship, but kept on fighting as they tumbled back to Earth.' Sir, it's right there in black-and-white."

"But not a single word of it's true," Dock scoffed, snatching the magazine from Nathaniel. "They have me jumping out of airplanes, fighting robots—" He opened to a random page and pointed to a passage. "Right here they got me trekking through the forest on some kind of rescue mission. It's all a bunch of horseshit," he cursed, tossing the pulp to the ground.

Lost for words, Nathaniel looked over to Gardner, pleading. For his part, Gardner leaned back, crossed his legs and took another sip of his drink. "True or not, Dock," he said, "thousands of kids have been eating it up for ten cents a pop every month for the past three years. *Ten* cents. Every month. There isn't another pulp out there with your kind of numbers. Hell, even *The Shadow* books aren't seeing pull like you. Remember that nice new Phantom III? Those books paid for it."

"*You* bought the Phantom III, Jimmy," Dock reminded him.

"Even so, the pulps—and hell, even the comics we got Siegel and Shuster doing over at National—got a limited lifespan. Boys grow up, they stop reading, and they discover girls; but where are they going to take the girls? Movies." He puffed his cigar. "We've talked about this, Dock. Serials; they're the next step you have to take if you want stay *relevant*. We don't make this jump now, we're gonna be on the street holding out paper cups."

Dock grimaced as he stood up and began to pace the room. Nathaniel struggled not to notice Dock's limp—they always hid it in the newsreels and *never* mentioned it in the pulps. "Look, it's not that I don't get what you're saying. The pulps and the comics are all well and good because at the end of the day they're not really me, just some words on a page and pictures that look nothing like me. But putting *me* on screen, that's different. Kids will start jumping off roofs to see if they can fly."

"But… is it really *that* different, sir?" Nathaniel ventured.

Dock raised a skeptical eyebrow, while Gardner bit back a smile and twirled his cigar encouragingly at Nathaniel.

"Go on, son," Gardner encouraged. "Tell him what you wanna say."

Nathaniel reached into his pocket and fished out his wallet, his hands shaking as he rummaged through the collection of dollars and papers. "Well, sir, I mean—what I *want* to say is… *Christ*," he stuttered as he brought out a small worn card. He held it up cautiously, a relic to be cherished. "Most guys my age used to walk around with this in our back pockets all the time for, y'know, good luck," he said, handing it to Dock.

Dock flipped the card over, knowing what it was before he looked at it: a colored drawing of him in his old uniform, mid-run; the number 24 in the lower left hand corner of the image; "Dock Doyle, 1st Base Chicago 'White Sox'" written across the bottom.

"Everyone in America considers you—" Nathaniel cut himself off. "I remember the papers calling you the '*Lincoln of Baseball*,' the 'Last, *Real* White Sox.' Hell, my dad used to talk about you like you were the Second Coming. And when you had the shoot out with Rothstein… All the girls on my block cried every day until they heard you were out of the hospital."

"Get to the point, kid," Dock said handing the card back to Nathaniel, his tone softer.

"Well, sir," Nathaniel said, wiping his brow with the back of his hand, "the *point* is the pulps… the serials… they're just an extension of what you already are: a legend. Sure, they're over-the-top, aggrandized versions of you, but they're still *you*: America's first *real* pulp hero."

A small smile curled the corner of Dock's lips. "How much they paying this kid, Jimmy?"

"A hundred dollars a week, sir," Nathaniel answered before Gardner could respond.

Dock lightly tapped Nathaniel on the shoulder. "They're not paying you enough," he said genuinely, but his eyes quickly steeled over. "However, my problems still stand. I'm not going to pretend to be something I'm not. And no matter what you say—" he looked sharply at Gardner "—or *anyone* says—I'm *no* pulp hero."

•••

"The March of Time!" Music swelled to a crescendo as a title card appeared. "Brooklyn Dodgers Sweep Yankees in 1941 'Subway' Series!"

"Euphoria rushes over Brooklyn as Dock Doyle's Dodgers win their third Series in five years," the announcer said over footage of the celebrating team. "Rookie Jackie Robinson hit the winning homerun in the ninth inning, sending the crowd into hysterics, chanting 'Rocket Robinson…'"

"It's too bad you weren't able to celebrate with them," Gardner whispered in the darkened theatre. It had been nearly two months since Dock had walked off the serial; two months of Gardner playing diplomat with the studio, of William Witney screaming on the phone; and two months of the tabloids eating up all the gossip they could find. Had it not been for Gardner's dragging him out to the theatre, Dock would have probably stayed locked up in his mansion until the studio system collapsed.

Dock shook his head. "They earned the spotlight, let them enjoy it; I would've just stolen it from them. Besides you see one World Series victory, you've seen them all."

"Yeah, I bet," Gardner said, taking a drag from his cigarette as they watched footage of Robinson being handed the MVP award. "I bet it gets boring *real* quick."

The newsreel's music took on a more a dire tone as a title card appeared: "*Germans Continue Invasion of Soviet Union*," eliciting audible boos from the audience. One kid was even bold enough to toss a box of candy at the screen when the newsreel cut to a shot of Hitler. Dock tried to ignore the twisting in his stomach at the beady-eyed visage of *der Führer,* as if he could hear the shattering glass of November nights. He shifted uncomfortably in his chair, his gaze dropping to his feet.

"They're thinking of replacing you with some guy named Tom Tyler," Gardner said casually. "He kind of looks like you; if you lost twenty pounds and if they fog up the lens."

"I ever see him in anything?"

Gardner thought for a moment then shook his head. "Probably not."

"I thought the whole point was 'they couldn't find anyone to play Dock Doyle, so they hired Dock Doyle himself.'"

"Yeah, well apparently Dock Doyle doesn't want to be *Dock Doyle*," Gardner retorted. "Far be it from me to question what rattles around in another man's head, but if you ask me, turning your back on the serials wasn't the brightest idea you've ever had."

"The conversation's over, Jimmy," Dock replied.

"Guess it is."

They watched as the rest of the newsreel in silence. The screen went black before a deep voice cried "SHAZAM!" followed instantly by the crash of the thunder. A big yellow lightning bolt flashed as a brightly colored title card appeared on screen, music blaring and triumphant. "Paramount Presents: A Max Fleischer Cartoon: Captain Marvel in Technicolor," it read, as the kids in the audience screamed with excitement.

"Would you look at that," Gardner scoffed, eyeing a young boy, no older than eight, bounce up and down in his seat. "If I didn't know better I would say the kid's head's about to pop. As if a kid could shout a word and become a man." He leaned over to Dock. "You know, if that actually worked I wouldn't've gone around saving the world. I would've gone straight to the closest bordello and tried out my new accessories." He took a drag from his cigarette. "You know, when Siegel and Shuster first came to National they pitched them something about some kind of alien hero. They almost bought it were it not the for the Dock Doyle property we sold them."

"What the hell is a hero anyway?" Dock mused, watching the boy. "I never wanted to do nothing but play ball. It's the only thing I was ever any good at. I didn't want to be 'Dock Doyle.'"

"There's no such thing as heroes, Dock," Gardner said as he watched young Billy Batson speak the Wizard's name and transform into Captain Marvel. "Not really, anyway. Just someone doing what's right by them at the right time for someone else. Nothing more than that. You just did what was right by you when Chick tried to bring you in on the fix, and for some reason, that sounded right to everybody else."

"Not everybody," Dock sighed, twisting the ring on his finger.

•••

Everything was darkness and fog; there were voices in the mist. How long had it been like this? Weeks? Months? It was all so muddled together now.

"Sir, I don't care who you are, you can't go in there! Mr. Doyle needs his rest!"

"Look sweetheart, I'll just be five minutes. Five minutes! Not even. Scout's honor. I just got to talk to him."

"Nurse," Dock croaked, his throat was so dry. It hurt to move. He cracked open his eyes, his hospital room was a multi-color blur. "Nurse, who is it?"

"It's some man, Mr. Doyle," the white blob said, slowly resolving into a young woman. "He says he's a friend."

Dock looked at the thin, grinning man. "Water," Dock instructed him.

The man quickly poured a glass, placed it against Dock's lips—it would be months before he could really move again—and carefully tilted the glass. Dock leaned his head forward as far as he could and took a sip.

"You've got two minutes," Dock whispered as the man placed the water on the bedside table.

"Name's James Gardner, but most call me Jimmy," the man said, taking off his hat, his light brown hair speckled with grey. He pulled a chair next to the Dock's hospital bed and sat down. "Mr. Doyle, I can't express my condolences enough. Everyone out there, we're all pulling for you."

Dock's bandaged face was unreadable.

Gardner nervously cleared his throat. "I have an idea for you, Mr. Doyle. Something that will inspire and make sure that your sacrifice wasn't in vain…"

•••

The sky was dark when they exited the theatre, the Los Angeles air dry and warm. A small crowd of fans, of all ages and sexes, flocked around Dock, waving pens and paper in his face, eager for signatures. Gardner stood off to the side as Dock diligently signed every piece of paper, shook every hand, hugged every sobbing woman, kissed every baby thrust before him; smiling warmly as he did. He would never understand why the public adored him as they did, but he knew it was these little moments that mattered most to them. It took nearly twenty minutes before everyone was appeased and the herd had cleared.

"Mr. Doyle?" a tall, redheaded British man said after the last fan drifted away. Bowler in hand, the Brit was smartly dressed, a thick mustache sitting above his upper lip, long sideburns bordering his face.

"I'm sorry, I don't have a pen," Dock quietly replied, patting his pockets. "I think I lost it in all the commotion, but if you have one, I'd be happy to sign."

The man smiled nervously and tugged his mustache. "No sir, I actually *don't* want an autograph. I have something very important to discuss with you."

Gardner stepped out from the shadows and moved between Dock and the other man. "I'm sorry, buddy, but Mr. Doyle is very busy," he said, placing a friendly, but firm, hand on the man's shoulder, pulling him away from Dock. "If you got something important to talk about you can make an appointment."

"It's about *Harold Dauer*, Mr. Doyle," the man added with urgency.

Dock's stomach tightened. "What did you say?"

"Harold Dauer," the British man reiterated. "A name that has some importance to you, if I'm not mistaken."

Gardner furrowed his brow. "Who the hell is he talking about?"

Dock waved away his agent's question and stepped toward the British man. "Maybe it does, but I'd like yours first," he demanded.

"Dr. Shane Tilston, chief archaeologist for the British Museum," he said with a smile as he sidestepped Gardner and extended a friendly hand.

"No offense, Dr. Tilston, but I find it a little odd someone such as yourself would associate with a thug like Harold."

Tilston allowed this with a soft chuckle. "Understandable; Harold is a ruffian and a scoundrel. Even so, I can assure you he has been a key asset to our endeavors. With your help, we can hopefully rescue him from his captors."

"Captors," Dock repeated, uncomfortable with the sound of it. "How did you know I was here? I don't exactly *publicize* my every move," he said, eyeing Gardner, who responded with an innocent shrug.

"Despite having an ocean and a continent between me and my home, I am not without my connections here," Tilston said proudly. He placed his bowler atop his head. "One of whom would very much like to talk with you," he added as a limousine pulled up to the curb besides him, almost on cue.

"Dock, I don't think you should buy what this limey's selling," Gardner warned.

"Mr. Doyle has handled the scum of the Earth, I'm certain he can handle this. Come, Mr. Doyle," Tilston quipped, "we can discuss this somewhere more comfortable."

•••

Dock had been in hundreds of mansions over the years—owned one himself—but this took the cake. Hundreds of rooms covering several acres, mahogany walls lined with paintings, ancient artifacts—from stone idols to golden masks—from across the globe. There were countless photos of celebrities and royalty, people who walked alongside history, shaping and molding the world. And somewhere, off in the distance, Dock could hear the faint buzzing of Los Angeles, forgotten like a drunken memory.

"This place has got to be twice the size of your place," Gardner observed. "Bigger, probably. You think this is a Lloyd Wright house? Damn, I can never tell."

"Where did all this come from?" Dock asked while he looked over a jewel-encrusted statuette of a falcon, unable to shake the feeling he had seen it before.

"All corners of the Earth," Tilston responded pleasantly. "Though unfortunately these items don't belong to me, or the British Museum, for that matter. They are part of a... *private* collection."

Gardner called from the other side of the room. "Hey, Dock, look at this."

Dock limped over. "It's a baseball bat," he observed.

"Not just *any* bat," Gardner said, tapping the metal plaque below the bat's casing.

Dock's eyes went wide in shock, and spun around to face Tilston. "Where the *hell* did you get this?"

The sound of heels against marble resounded as a tall, beautiful, brunette walked into the room. "I see you've found your game-winning bat from the infamous '19 World Series," the woman said, her eyes locked on Dock. Her accent spoke of royalty, her lips seemingly frozen in a knowing smirk.

"Check out the *looker*," Gardner whispered.

"From what I've been told it was a stunning game," the woman continued, "even without all the intrigue associated with it. As to how I have the bat— Well, let's just say I have my *sources*. Lady Donna Donovan," she replied to the unspoken question. "It is so exciting to finally meet you, Mr. Doyle. Your fame precedes you even in London. It is such a rare pleasure to be in the company of such an unparalleled man. And Mr. Gardner, I've heard quite a bit about you as well."

Gardner gave her a warm smile. "Hopefully nothing you can prove or my wife would have my head. One of them, at least."

"Why don't you cut the bullshit and tell me what happened to Harold," Dock said, his patience wearing thin.

Donovan pursed her lips. "Straight to business then."

Tilston stepped forward. "Mr. Doyle, have you ever heard of the 'Wandering City?'" he asked rhetorically as he unfurled a large roll of yellowed paper over the large billiard table, revealing an ancient map of South America. The continent's proportions and coastlines were malformed, the borders vague. Towards the southern tip Dock saw a small illustration of a city, the words *Ciudad de los Césares* scribbled beneath it. "Also known as the 'City of the Caesars,' it is a mythical city supposedly located in an Andes valley somewhere in the southern region of South America known as Patagonia, here," he pointed to the small illustration. "According to most accounts, the city is full of treasure. One even claims it is located between a mountain of gold and another of diamonds—though I think it's safe to say that is utter hogwash. Some believe the city was placed under a spell and only appears at certain times. As to who lives there, the answer varies. From descendents of the Incan Empire to survivors of the shipwrecks in the Strait of Magellan, to the more fantastic such as giants and ghosts, but—"

"Skip to the part where you tell me what this has to do with Harold," Dock interrupted, not buying a word of it.

Tilston stole a glance at Donovan.

"Harold was a scout for our... *expedition*," Donovan replied after a moment.

"Expedition?" Dock sputtered in disbelief. "You mean you actually believe this crap?"

"Believe? No. Don't be ridiculous," Donovan scoffed, waving a dismissive hand over the map. "These are all myths and legends, stories of fancy like Atlantis or El Dorado. But in every story there is a kernel of truth and we believe there once *was* a city in Patagonia, perhaps some sort of lost civilization. We sent Harold down there a month ago to see if there was any truth to the legends."

"What went wrong?"

Reaching into his jacket pocket, Tilston brought out a folded piece of paper and handed it to Dock. "We received this two days ago."

Gardner shifted over next to Dock as he unfolded the letter and looked over it, but Dock only shrugged, unable to read it.

"It's Spanish," Tilston explained, taking back the letter. "From Harold's kidnappers. In short, they demand ten thousand dollars or they will kill him."

Dock let out a sardonic laugh and started walking out towards the hallway. "And let me guess you want me to pay? I grew up alongside pickpockets and conmen. I know a *scam* when I see one," he said as he exited the room.

As Dock rounded the corner, Tilston and Donovan looked at Gardner in panic. He massaged his eyes and gave them a frustrated shrug that seemed to say: "This is how he is."

Tilston reached into his jacket pocket and handed Donovan a rolled up handkerchief. "Show it to him before he gets away," he urged.

"Mr. Doyle!" Donovan called after Dock, the sound of her heels on marble echoing down the hall. "Mr. Doyle, please, listen! This is *not* a scam." She ran up beside him, pleading. "I beg you. We don't want your money. We want you to help us *rescue* him."

Dock bit back a snarl. "Rescue?" He spun around and grabbed her by the arm. Gritting his teeth, he leaned forward, his face less than an inch from hers. "Don't try and play me," he hissed. "Someone drops the name Harold Dauer in front of me, they know something most people *don't*. So start talking or I'm walking to the nearest police station and reporting you and your tall friend back there. And trust me, it won't matter if you're the *goddamn* Queen of England; when I say jump the whole nation leaps."

"I… I understand, Mr. Doyle," Donovan stuttered nervously, her arm beginning to throb under Dock's vise-like grip. "But you see— The kidnappers— They didn't just send us a letter. They also sent us this," she said, opening her clenched hand to reveal the rolled handkerchief, a shriveled severed finger inside, the nail sliced in half.

•••

Fumbling through his study, Dock found the small brass key stuffed in the bottom desk drawer, buried under a pile of papers and folders. Stuffing the key into his pocket, he dragged a chair up over to the bookshelf in the furthest corner and stepped up, blindly patting the dusty surface until his hand landed on a small tin box. Sliding it towards him with the tips of his fingers, he grabbed the box and placed it on the floor. He kneeled in front of it, his hands shaking so badly it took him three tries before he was able to unlock the latch. Staring down at the contents—the worn

"Check out the looker," Gardner whispered.

book, the faded photographs, the circular piece of suede—Dock reached into his jacket pocket and brought out a small matchbox. Striking a match, its tiny flame casting heavy shadows across the darkened room, he dropped it into the tin box, watching the contents smolder for several minutes before igniting.

An hour later, all that remained was ash.

•••

Far outside Los Angeles, stars pinpricked the sky; the Hollywoodland sign was lost to the horizon. Sitting at the end of the private airfield, the new Boeing Model 307 Stratoliner gleamed in the moonlight, its propeller engines silent, begging to taste air; two large capital "D's" painted on the tail, presumably for "Donna Donovan."

"I don't like it, Dock. Something doesn't add up," Gardner said as their car pulled up to the airfield. "Not that I want to, but I should go with you,"

"You need to be here for Mary and the kids," Dock said, staring out at the airplane, his expression unreadable. "You've got enough strikes against you, she'd kill you if you left. Besides, I need you to keep the studio off my back while I'm away."

Gardner shook his head. "You shouldn't trust these people, Dock."

"I don't," Dock said as he put on his fedora and opened the door.

Gardner placed a hand on his shoulder. "Come on, Dock, this is ridiculous. How long have we known each other?"

Dock sighed, but kept his back turned to Gardner "There's a lot of things I don't want people to know about me—that I don't want *you* to know. I need you to respect that."

"What can be so bad you can't tell me?"

"Go home, Jimmy," Dock said as he stepped out onto the runway.

"At least tell me who's Harold Dauer," he begged.

But Dock just slammed the door shut and limped towards the plane.

Moments later, Gardner took a long drag of his cigarette as he watched the plane take off into the night sky. The whirring sound of the propellers disappeared into the darkness.

"Home, Mr. Gardner?" the driver asked.

"Not yet," Gardner replied. "Republic Studios. There's someone I need to see."

•••

Uneasy hours passed into restless days. Dock slept little—and only in fits and spurts, dreams filled of voices and eyes. The plane made stops in Panama City and Santiago before finally arriving in the small city of Punta Arenas at the southern edge of Chile. There they transferred to a small yacht, the *Bonita*, captained by a tiny native man named Nehuen. Chewing tobacco permanently planted in his jaw, he told Dock to call him: *"En*, like the letter, *si?"*

They began making their way back north through the straits, towards the mountain group known as *Cordillera del Paine*. The tides pushed and pulled, tilting the boat in long, swaying motions, the boat's engine humming. Night fell, bringing with it a black cloud threatening rain.

Dock sat alone in his cabin, barefoot in his khakis and shirt, idly twirl-ing the chamber of his revolver over and over before snapping it into place. *Spin, click!* He had never loved the feel of guns, hated the smell of gunpowder, loathed the sound of the shot, and when the bullet found its target— *Spin, click!* But Gardner was right, things didn't add up. Everything fit together well enough, until you started looking closely and the holes started to grow, and the whole story started to fall apart. *Spin, click!* But, this wasn't just some back alley scam; this was something bigger. These people were after something, but what? *Spin, click!*

He remembered the sound of gunfire and his mind slipped back two decades.

•••

"I don't care how much it is, I don't want it." Dock said, ignoring the slight twist of his stomach as he tossed the wad of cash back on the table. He looked up at the eight other players, all clumped together, save for Shoeless Joe Jackson who stood off in the shadows. "You do what you want, but count me out."

Chick Gandil rubbed his jaw, his beady, callous eyes burning into Dock. "If you ain't in on this, then we got a problem."

Dock shook his head. "Only if you want to make it one."

Gandil stepped forward, his muscular six-two frame towering over Dock's five-eight. "Believe me, Doyle," he growled as he pocketed the cash. "I'm not the one you gotta be worryin' about."

Two weeks later, Gandil's threat proved true.

"Look, the Boss is giving you this warning in consideration of who your family is," the gangster said as he slid off his bloodied brass knuckles. "Besides, I've seen you play, you got talent. Don't waste it trying to be all high 'n mighty. Got me? Straighten up. I don't wanna have to mess up that pretty bride of yours."

He stumbled home blindly, one eyelid puffed and purple. He dragged himself up the steps to the entrance, knocking his head against the door as he passed out from the pain.

"What are you going to do?" Rachel asked him as she cleaned the blood off his face hours later.

"What would you want me to do?" he asked in reply, looking at her with his one good eye, his voice betraying his desperation.

She frowned, running the faucet over the bloodied cloth, her gaze drifting over to the quiet crib in the bedroom.

Two days later Dock bought a gun—a Colt revolver like in the Westerns—despite Rachel's trepidation. He would carry it with him everywhere outside his home, save for when he was on the field. It was the only place he ever felt truly safe.

Dock didn't like Comiskey—no one did—but if anyone could end it, it was him: The owner of the White Sox.

"Those thieving bastards," Comiskey cursed, drumming his fingers on his desk. "Those little pieces of shit. How long has this been going on?"

"I don't know, sir. They only just tried to bring me in."

"Eight men," Comiskey rubbed his eyes. These were his best players. "Even Jackson?"

Dock nodded.

"Fuck."

The press ate it up. There was nothing quite like a good scandal, and this one topped them all. Dock's face could be seen on every newsstand from New York to San Francisco. Photographers and newspapermen camped outside his home, mobbing him and Rachel whenever they dared leave. They kept the windows drawn, but even then, they knew they were being watched.

"What would you want me to do?" Dock asked Rachel again, his voice barely a whisper; their hands intertwined.

She let out a long sigh and looked him the eyes. "Well, you were always good with a bat."

Dock swung with all his strength, feeling the weight of the world on his back. The ball launched into the sky like a rocket, hitting its apex over the bleachers. As he watched it fall beyond the edge of the park he realized he could barely hear the roar of the crowd. He dropped his bat and headed for first.

It was October 9th. The final score was 6-5.

Even with eight men out, the White Sox had won the Series.

Dock had always refused to have a driver. A real man should drive himself, he said. They were going out to celebrate, not the Series—the Series felt like a distant memory at this point. It was his son Richie's first birthday.

He turned a corner. Two big black sedans were parked across the middle of the street, another pulled up behind him. Dock could see about four of Rothstein's men in each.

Rothstein got out of the car on the right, his hands in his pockets. "Come out, Little D. Time we talked."

Dock's eyes dropped to his feet, he knew what it meant. He took his gun from his shoulder holster and checked the cartridges. Just enough to put up a fight.

He looked at Rachel and then to Richie in her arms. "Stay down. Don't get up unless I tell you." He reached for the door.

"Don't," she whispered, pulling at his sleeve as if it would stop him.

He pressed his hand to her cheek and found strength in her eyes. "Don't get up unless I tell you," he reiterated as he stepped out of the car.

When he woke from his coma they told him over fifty bullets had been fired, fifteen people dead, but only two that mattered.

•••

Dock could feel his eyes start to sting, and tried to fight back the tears. He had only tried to do what he had thought was *right*, prove he was better than what he was. If only he had known things would have gone so terribly wrong— If he had only known the cost.

There was a knock on the door pulling him back to the present.

"One minute," he called, slipping the Colt under his pillow and wiping his eyes with the back of his hand. Limping over, he opened the door to find Lady Donovan, her white nightgown hinting at the mysteries underneath.

"Up late, Mr. Doyle?" Donovan asked with a coy smile. "I saw the light coming from under the door."

"A little late to be walking around."

"No rest for the wicked, they say," she laughed, but Dock's face remained unmoved. "I just wanted to make sure you were comfortable. See if you got your sea legs. I know the accommodations aren't *quite* what you're used to," she said with a smile, "but if there's anything you need, please let me *know*."

Dock gave her a silent nod and nothing else.

Donovan looked him over for a moment, her gaze penetrating. "You're such a quiet man," she breathed.

Dock shrugged. "Don't have much to say."

She crossed her arms, studying him. "You're nothing like I expected, Mr. Doyle, but then I suppose we live our life based on assumptions and expectations, only to see them continually turned on their heads. But you— I expected a loudmouth. Someone so completely driven by their own ego that there was little room for anything else."

"Sorry to disappoint."

"No disappointment at all," she said. "A woman with my upbringing is constantly surrounded by suitors, men who jabber on and on about all their achievements and victories. It becomes quite *boring* after you've heard so many tales of adventure and excitement, knowing not a word of which is true. But you, you are a *mystery* aren't you?" Her voice lowered to a whisper as she inched closer. Dock could feel her breath against his lips. It had been so long… would it really be so bad? "For all your name has given you, all of that is really just the skin of it, containing so much more below—" Her hand touched his arm, pulling at his sleeve. Her lips brushed against his. "How I wonder what I'll find—"

Dock placed his hands on her shoulders and pushed her away. "I think you should leave."

Donovan looked at him in a mix of confusion and surprise, as if he had strayed from the script. "I—" she stuttered and cleared her throat, her eyes catching the white gold band on his finger. "I didn't mean to—"

"Leave," he said with a slight nod.

Her eyes welling up, Donovan hurried away as Dock closed the door behind her. Dock walked over to the sink at the other end of the room and splashed water on his face when he caught his reflection in the small dirty mirror. Beneath the stony, distant expression he recognized the eyes of a young man from the Brooklyn, whose dreams lived in the wood of a bat and the leather of a mitt. Dock grimaced. He didn't know that kid anymore. He ran his wet palm across the silvered glass, twisting the reflection.

As he dried his face he heard a soft creak as his door opened. Dock sighed. "I *thought* I told you to lea—" He looked up into the mirror and saw through the mirror's wet distortion a small, painted man unsheathe a blade. "Shit."

Dock spun around as the painted man raised the blade above his head and screeched: "Yai! Yai!"

•••

The blade sliced across Dock's arm and chest, tearing open his shirt, bringing forth a thin line of crimson. Dock grunted trying to ignore the pain as he threw a powerful fist at his attacker's head. The painted man had anticipated this and subtly leaned back, sending Dock's punch wild. As Dock stumbled forward the native spun around, cutting Dock's upper back. Dock screamed as excruciating pain shot up his spine. But the native wasn't done with him yet. Wrapping his arm around Dock's neck, he squeezed down, closing on Dock's windpipe like a living vise. His vision blurred, Dock dug his fingers into the native's arm, drawing blood. Ignoring Dock's efforts, the painted man growled as he pressed his blade against Dock's cheek, drawing blood.

With oxygen deprivation taking hold, Dock was rapidly running out of options. With all his remaining strength, Dock jabbed his elbow into the painted man's side. As the native screamed, the telltale sound of a cracking rib could be heard. The painted man's grip loosened as he stumbled back. Freed, Dock reeled forward onto his cot, his hand sliding under the pillow, feeling cold steel caressing his fingertips. Without a moment to lose, Dock grabbed the revolver and spun, squeezing the trigger before the painted man could react. There was a loud *crack* as the bullet struck the painted man in the jaw, sliced up through his head and exploded out the back of his skull. Blood and bone splattered out across the mirror looking more like strawberry preserves than brain matter. The painted man's knees buckled and the corpse collapsed into a motionless heap of meat.

His breath ragged, his head and lungs still screaming, Dock forced his way to his feet. His hands shook as he stared at the body, watching crimson pool out onto the deck, unconsciously taking a step back as it neared his toes. Something moved in the corner of his eyes but when he looked up all he saw was his reflection, covered in blood.

Where there was one, there were more.

Dock risked a glance through the doorway, finding the hallway empty; the only sounds the whirring of the engine and the rush of the waves resonating through the walls. Sliding out of his cabin, Dock kept the gun raised, his eyes darting left and right as he limped down the narrow hall. The exit to the starboard deck was open, swinging back and forth with the roll of the ship squeaking like a screaming rodent as rain began to fall outside. Dock took a tentative step out into the darkness, the stormy black waves dancing against the bulkhead. His heart hammering in his throat, the hard rain quickly soaking him head to toe, he took another step, the wet deck cold against his bare feet. Dock stopped short; there was something beneath the sounds of rain, waves and engine. He peered into the shadows. He could hear someone breathing—

"Help me—" someone whispered. Dock whipped left as Donovan stumbled out, a second painted man pressing a jagged stone blade against her thin neck, drawing blood. Donovan moaned in pain, tears streaming down her cheeks, mixing with the rain. "Please!"

The native began to curse in his foreign tongue as Dock raised his revolver and—*BAM!*

Donovan screamed as brain and bone splattered against the hull, the native's face collapsing inward. The stone blade fell loose from his hand as the body slipped back, smacking against the deck with a wet *thunk!*

"Holy Christ!" Donovan exclaimed, collapsing to her knees. She held her right ear in pain, the native's blood covering half her face. "You shot him!" she screamed. "You actually bloody shot him!"

Dock knelt down in front of Donovan, placing a hand on her shoulder. She was shivering. "Where are the others?"

"My ear! It's all ringing!" she screeched. "I can't hear anything!"

"Yes, you can," Dock told her. "Listen to me. I need to find Tilston and the ship's crew before it's too late."

Donovan eyes were vacant, looking right through Dock. "You didn't even *say* anything," she said to herself, her voice rising in pitch as she neared hysterics. Dock could feel gooseflesh form on her bare shoulders, her body shivering. "You just pointed and shot!"

Dock scowled. There was no time for this. "Listen!" he exclaimed, slapping Donovan hard across the face, taking no pleasure in the act. "Where are Tilston and En?!"

A large red handprint began to form on Donovan's cheek. She looked at Dock as if he had appeared from thin air. "In the… In the cockpit… I think… I saw them there—"

Dock jumped up and raced toward the bow of the ship. "Get inside a cabin quick and lock the door," he commanded. "Go! Go now!"

As Dock raced away, Donovan silently wrapped her arms around herself, turning her body away from the corpse, unable to look at it as blood spilled out from the native's shattered skull and the rain washed it away. Her teeth began to chatter. "This is all going *wrong*!"

•••

Dock charged down the ship, keeping to the shadows as best he could. How many natives had come aboard? Five? Ten? More? There were four bullets remaining in his revolver, enough to put up a fight, but not save the day. No matter what the pulps and comics might say, Dock was afraid of dying. He had seen death up close, felt life slip away in his arms. He didn't want to face the Reaper, not now, not ever, not until he was ready. And he certainly wasn't ready now.

Crouching down, Dock slide underneath the cockpit window, holding his breath as he listened to murmurs echoing from within. He couldn't make out the words but there were two, maybe three voices. One was deep—Tilston—the other was slightly higher, quick and rhythmic. It sounded familiar, but that was impossible— He heard a door slam and they all fell silent.

Dock chewed the inside of his cheek as he checked his revolver again. Four rounds, he reminded himself. *Dammit.* Why hadn't he grabbed more bullets? *A rookie mistake*, his dad would've said in that gravelly, accented voice.

He needed to look inside, it wasn't enough to *hear* them, he needed to know how many there were, how bad the odds were, before he went and did something stupid. He could almost feel Rachel's hand touch his arm. *Don't.*

"I can't sit by and do nothing," he whispered as though she was sitting next to him. "Just be brave for me."

Dock closed his eyes and took a deep breath. He had been strong for her, now he needed to be strong for himself. He quickly peeked through the window. Three and two. Two loin-clothed natives, one with a serrated blade, one with a blowgun in hand; on the ground, Tilston, En and a crewmember. Tilston and the others were beaten and scared, but alive. This was good; the odds were currently in their favor. All Dock needed was to take one native down and the other could be overpowered. Dock wiped the rain from his eyes and pulled back the revolver's hammer. No time like the present.

Dock kicked open the door with his good leg, sending the world into madness. Time seemed to fold over itself, slow down and speed up all at once. The natives were shouting. The captives were screaming. One native ran forward, raising his blade. There was a quiet puff of air and a quick whistle. Dock ducked out of instinct. A small wooden dart hit against the bulkhead, dropping to the ground with a fairy-like *dink-dink*. There were two quick shots, the sound echoing and deafening in the small space. Tilston screamed, covering his ears. The door flapped shut with the shifting of the boat. Blood sprayed out from the bullet holes in the native's chest and stomach. Dock leaped at the native with the blowgun, tackling him to the ground as he struck him across the head with the revolver and knocking him unconscious. The knife-wielding native slammed against the wall of the cockpit, sliding down to the deck, leaving a streak of blood behind him as his vacant stare met Tilston's. Dock could hear Tilston whisper, "Don't break. Don't break. Don't break." The boat rocked again and the door flew open, waves of rain sprinkling through, time unfolded and moved in one direction again. Sweat and remnants of the rain poured down Dock's forehead, his breathing heavy. He could feel his heart hammer hard against his ribcage—he was no longer a young man.

Dock holstered his revolver and wiped his forehead with the back of his arm. He walked over to the dead native and pulled free the stone blade before turning to Tilston. "Are you okay?" Dock asked, and when he didn't receive a reply, "Doctor Tilston, are you all right?"

Tilston pulled his gaze from the native's dead eyes. Swallowing the lump in his throat, he nodded. "Yes," he croaked as Dock cut off his bindings. "Yes. I think we are—"

Dock sighed with relief. "Are there any more?"

Dock leaped at the native, he struck him across the head.

"No," Tilston shook his head, grimacing as though he had forgotten something. He closed his eyes for a moment. "I mean… Yes. There were… three of them. The third left. I don't know where he is. They snuck into our cabins and brought us here."

"Four," Dock corrected, moving to release En and the other crewmember, helping them to their feet. "One came into my cabin, the other attacked Donovan."

Tilston pulled himself up, leaning heavily against the wall as he chewed this over. "You think they were with the kidnappers?"

Dock studied him for a moment. "Crossed my mind."

Tilston nodded, rubbing his chin while watching the rain drum against the windshield. "What happened to them? The other men who attacked you—" he asked, his voice just above a whisper.

Dock let his silence answer the question.

Tilston sighed, shaking his head mournfully. "Messy situation isn't it?"

"Wasn't pretty," Dock replied with a shake of his head as he helped En off the floor.

"No," Tilston whispered, gazing out the window as if someone were looking back. He turned to Dock after a moment. "No, I suppose it wouldn't be." He ran his hand through his hair. "Where is Lady Donovan?

"Alive."

"Thank God," Tilston said with a nod as if he had already known the answer. He looked over at Dock whose wounds had turned his white undershirt a deep maroon. "You're injured."

"I've had worse," Dock replied with a shrug, using his belt as an impromptu sheath for the stone blade.

"What do we do now?" Tilston asked.

Dock thrust his chin at the unconscious native. "We make him talk."

•••

The forest echoed silence, as though the creatures of the jungle had retreated into the shadows before their advance. It had been two days since the attack on the *Bonita*. They had waited until morning to dispose of the bodies, tossing them over the side without memorial, though Dock could tell, of all of them, Tilston seemed the most upset, wearing an expression that hinted at guilt. They roused the surviving native soon after. Bound to a small chair in the galley, the native awoke in panic, pulling at the ropes while he yelled in his unintelligible tongue. If there was ever a killer behind those watery orbs, it had been washed away by the rain last night. After several moments of screaming, Tilston asked Dock to step out.

"You understand what he's saying?" Dock asked incredulously.

Tilston nodded. "I'll see what I can get out of him. Five minutes. That should hopefully be enough."

Dock chewed the inside of his cheek as he considered the sobbing native. "Five minutes," he told Tilston. "That's all you get."

Tilston nodded, understanding Dock's implication. In six minutes, it would be

Dock's turn, and there was no assurance the native would survive the interrogation. Dock spent the next four minutes reloading and unloading his revolver, listening to the murmurs of hushed conversation and not understanding a word of it. As the last minute wound down, Dock replaced the last bullet and pulled back the hammer as Tilston exited, his hands shaking. The doctor whispered: "We have our heading."

Would Harold have done all this for him? Dock wondered as he sliced through the brush. Would he have gone this far, pushed into the deepest, darkest parts of South America hoping to save the person who had all but disowned him? Dock could feel a snarl form on his lips; there was a rage building inside him. What would he do when he saw Harold again?

"Mr. Doyle! We must rest," Tilston called from several feet away, holding up Donovan by her waist. She was shaking from exhaustion; sweat running down her narrow frame. Her left ear was bandaged, her hearing still damaged, but improving.

"Tell him to stop, Shane," she whispered. "Please… just for a little while…"

But Dock kept pushing forward, chopping at the overgrowth with single-minded ferocity. Watching the former sports hero, the Lincoln of Baseball, tear through the jungle with such savagery was simply heartbreaking. To have done so many great things with one's life and to end up here played like a pawn on a chessboard. Eyeing the subtle movement in the woods around them, Tilston could barely hide his frown.

"Please, Mr. Doyle!" Tilston said, exhaustion raking his body. "Lady Donovan isn't well."

Dock stopped and weakly swung his machete at a branch, his massive shoulders rising and falling in a long, defeated motion as he slowly turned back to face them. Sweat poured down his face, his white shirt stained with yellow half circles. He glanced up at the sky, squinting as he measured the sun. Nodding he said in a gruff, worn voice. "For a little while." He stepped over and cleared off the top of a fallen tree. "We don't want to be lost in the dark."

"I'm not sure how much further we have to go," Tilston said as he handed Dock a canteen a short while later. "I've tried to keep track of our position as best I can, but with all these trees, I'm not even certain we've been moving in a straight line or going in circles."

Dock took a swig from the canteen and nodded over at Donovan, her gaze digging into the ground. "How is her hearing?" he asked.

"Getting better," Tilston replied, "as far as I can tell."

"I didn't mean to hit her," Dock whispered as he handed back the canteen. "I would never—" He squeezed his eyes shut, hunting for the words but finding only regret. "There is no excuse."

Tilston lifted the canteen to his mouth and noticed his hands were shaking. Grimacing, he replaced the cap and put it back into his satchel. Patting his shirt pockets he found his packet of cigarettes and drew out a soggy stick. "Cig?" he asked, offering one to Dock.

"Don't smoke," Dock replied with a subtle wave.

"Heh," Tilston laughed, the sound hollow to his ears. "Neither did I until I started this job."

"You've worked for Donovan long?" Dock inquired, the tone of his voice making it plain he didn't care if Tilston answered or not.

"Long enough," Tilston murmured in reply as he struggled to light his cigarette. A glimmer caught his eyes, shining from between the trees. Panic boiled up from his stomach. Did Dock see it? He risked a glance over at the ballplayer, if he had seen anything, his stony expression didn't betray this. Tilston opened and closed his hands trying unsuccessfully to stop the shaking, the cigarette hanging from his lips, forgotten. There was no question in his mind what was going to happen next, it had been so well planned, so well scripted, it all moved like clockwork.

And it was wrong.

"Mr. Doyle… Dock." Tilston lost his voice for a moment as he felt Dock's gaze fall upon him. "Before we go any further— There's something I need to tell you— Something you should know." He froze as Dock placed a hand on his shoulder and quietly drew his revolver.

Dock pressed a finger to his lips. *I hear something.* He stood and cautiously approached the brush. Squeezing his eyes shut, Tilston let out a quavering sigh. He pulled out his sidearm, already knowing what was going to happen.

Birds burst out from the treetops as gunfire shattered the silence, their caws drowning out the screams.

It was over in an instant, a mere blur of motion and blood, leaving four natives dead on the ground; a fifth native, shot through the leg, lay crumpled at their feet, futilely trying to stave the crimson flow from his wound. A sixth had run away at the behest of his compatriots. Donovan sat sobbing several feet away, her fragile grip on sanity slipping perilously through her fingertips. The brash woman Tilston had met in the small office all those months ago was gone, replaced with a whimpering child. They had never been prepared for all this death. If they had only known the cost, they would have never agreed to this ruse.

"Ask him where their base camp is," Dock demanded of Tilston, his voice hoarse but terrifying even as he reloaded his revolver.

Tilston kept his eyes on the ground. Had Dock Doyle always been so callous? He tried to remember all the newsreels he had seen over the years, the tall, handsome man smiling at the cameras, teeth so white they were glowing spots on the screen. All those kids, pulps tucked in their back pockets, jumping around alternating between pretending to be the "Last, Real White Sox" and "Doctor Dread." Was the man those kids—the whole nation—looked up to really a cold-blooded killer? Tilston felt his eyes tighten. Who was Dock Doyle, really?

"Dr. Tilston, are you going to ask him or not?" Dock asked, his voice a razor's edge.

Tilston heard himself speak to the young native boy—he couldn't be more than sixteen—apologizing for what was happening, this wasn't what he had thought it was going to be. The boy rambled back, begging, pleading, asking why, why, over and over again, why? "Because," Tilston replied in the native's tongue, unconcerned whether Dock understood a word of what they said, "there are very greedy men in this world, and like you, I am their pawn."

The boy's expression tightened in anger and in a hushed breath made a promise. The others would come, he swore, and the forest would run red with the blood of the transgressors.

"I hope that's true," Tilston replied. "Because we do not deserve mercy."

The boy's face slackened with bewilderment and blood loss, his skin already growing paler. Tilston watched the ground beneath the boy grow ever darker; his eyes roll up in his head, while he wobbled back and forth. The bullet had pierced the femoral artery. It would all be over soon. As the boy fell forward with heavy *thud*, Tilston looked to Dock and simply said: "Okay."

• • •

They moved further into the brush, the hot sun beat down on them; tree branches scratched their arms, pulling small tears into their shirts. Dock felt outside his body, as if he was watching a film of himself, running through the projector with broken spools, stuttering and flashing, skipping scenes and dialogue. There was gunfire and screams, blood and sweat. Dock's hand burned from the heat of his gun, remembering the old sting from those early days, before the game became his life. Seven kills with eight bullets. Wouldn't his father be proud? His father, who had never touched a gun himself, using a small army of men to deal out death like a Gatling gun; but Dock had always been his favorite weapon, calling him Goliath. There were nights when Dock would stumble home, blood caking his hands. His father would grip Dock's shoulders, his eyes brimming with tears of pride, digging his fingers into the muscle. "My boy," he'd whisper. "The giant killer."

His father. How long had it been since Dock had thought of that man, his long white beard, two strips of gray running down from the sides of his mouth; always tugging on it while he thought or spoke, as if he needed the reminder it was still attached. It was with some irony then that he never placed his fingers near his beard the last time Dock saw him.

• • •

"No," the old man said, lacing his arthritic fingers together as he studied the couple. "No, that will not do."

Dock furrowed his brow, his hand instinctually reaching for Rachel's, his heart in his throat. "What do you mean?"

The old man shook his head. "This pairing," he replied with a dismissive wave, his accent so thick it sank to the ground like cold air. "I cannot approve it."

Dock shifted forward in his chair, lips firming into an angry white line. "But father—"

The old man's eyes became daggers, his voice threatening to boil over with anger. "I have said all there is to say on the matter."

"All there is to say?" Dock shot to his feet. Rachel placed a placating hand on his arm, but Dock pulled it away, slamming his fist on the old man's massive wooden desk, knocking down a seven-branched candelabrum. "All there is to say!? I'm your son, *dammit.* You tell me why!"

The old man studied Dock as he replaced the candelabra. "No," he said after a moment. He looked to the short man standing in the shadows behind Dock. "Escort them out."

The short man, with black hair like Dock's, but with his mother's chin and nose, his right middle finger slightly deformed, the nail sliced in half, stepped forward and took Dock by the arm. "Time to go"

"Don't touch me," Dock growled, ripping the short man's hand away as he stepped up to the old man's desk. "I've sacrificed everything for you. Everything I've ever wanted—" Dock met the old man's immovable yellow, glaucomic eyes and let out a heavy, exasperated sigh. "Dammit, why am I even trying? This is it. I'm done with you. I'm done with all of this."

The old man pursed his lips and looked over and gave the short man a subtle nod. The meeting was over. His anger boiling over, Dock swept his hand across the desk, scattering the litany of books and pens onto the floor in a clattering avalanche while the old man watched, unfazed.

Dock spit, leaving a wet, yellow wad on the old man's lapel. "Tamut," Dock cursed as his eyes met the old man's one final time, finding nothing. "Let's go," he said taking Rachel by the hand as they left the narrow office, the short man following after them.

"Don't be like this," the short man pleaded in a hushed voice. "We can fix this; you just need to calm down."

"The old man made his decision, there's no reason to fight it. You know I've got a Chinaman's chance at making him change his mind," Dock said as he kept on walking towards the exit.

"Come on, don't be dumb," the short man grabbed Dock's shoulder. "You walk away now he's gonna cut you off; you're done. There ain't no going back."

Dock glanced back over his shoulder. "And what about you?" he asked.

The short man furrowed his brow, taken aback by this. He quietly replied: "You know where I stand, brother." He stole a glance at Rachel. "Tell me is the pussy really worth—"

Dock spun around, his face red with anger as he slammed the short man against the wall. "You watch your tongue. You call Rachel that again; I'll rip it out of your mouth. You get me?" The small man gave him a curt nod. "Just because you follow him like a lost puppy doesn't mean I have to. I'm tired of living my life as if I were still under his roof. He pretends to be a man of God when he's nothing but a petty thug. Well, I'm going to show him I'm more than that."

"Both of you," Rachel quietly interjected. "Stop it."

"Fine," the short man said, brushing down his suit. "What are you gonna do now?"

Dock shrugged. "I dunno, Harold. I've always been good with a bat."

•••

"Mr. Doyle?" Tilston's voice came through the darkness of mem-ories. "Mr. Doyle, I think we're here," he said, pushing aside a dense branch to reveal a small, deserted village, stout wooden huts sat in a semicircle, silent guardians of a lost civilization. The air tasted different here, Dock thought. It wasn't the old, moss-covered smell that permeated the jungle; this had the taste of gasoline, sawdust and metal. At the center of the semicircle, in a small wooden cage, was a narrow white man with black hair like Dock's but thinner now, speckled with gray, pushing the forehead back. The nose that had looked like their mother's was broken, turned left and flattened.

"David!" Harold scrambled forward, reaching his bone-thin arms through the wooden bars. Black circles lined his blood-red eyes. "Oh God, David, I'm so sorry."

Dock's heart hammered into his throat as he ran forward, sliding toward the cage like he was stealing second. "Harold. Harold, shut up, okay?" Dock whispered, pulling out the stone knife. "Just stay quiet; I'll get you out of this."

"I'm so sorry, David," Harold sobbed, tears cutting through the dirt on his face while Dock began hacking at one of the wooden bars. "I didn't mean for it to be like this. I tried, David. I really did."

Dock shook his head as he looked over the bars. "Shh, shh—"

"It was just that it was so hard after Dad. Things were so bad—"

"Harold, I'm going to get you out but I need you to stop talking, you understand?" Dock said as calmly as he could manage.

Harold reached out and grabbed Dock's arm. "Dammit, David. It's so good to see you."

"My name's Dock," he corrected, removing Harold's arm. "It's Dock now. Just calm down, I'll cut you free—" Dock stopped short, his eyes falling on Harold's bound hands and the slightly deformed middle finger, the nail sliced in half. Dock could feel his lungs threatening collapse. "Your hand," he whispered, dropping the stone knife.

"What?" Harold asked, his voice betraying his panic.

"Mr. Doyle, what are you doing?" Tilston called from the brush. "Cut him loose before—!"

"He has ten fingers!" Dock hollered, forcefully grabbing Harold's five-digit hand and pulling him against the wooden bars, knocking open a narrow opening. "Harold has ten fingers!"

"Oh bloody hell," Tilston breathed, his eyes wide as he stumbled back. He looked at Donovan in panic. "Oh *shit*."

Then from forest, Dock heard a familiar voice echo out: "CUT!"

•••

"Looks like we're gonna have to fire that special effects artist," Jimmy Gardner said as he walked out from behind the brush, his smile, loose and easy, shining in the bright southern sunlight. He was wearing a khaki safari suit, worn and dirty

"He has ten fingers!" Dock hollered.

from an extended trip through the forest. He casually wiped the sweat from his brow. "I have to say, Dock, you always prove to be smarter than I give you credit for."

"Jimmy?" Dock's throat tightened as he fell to his knees. He watched in horror as William Witney, the screenwriter Nathaniel Wharton—along with an army of men carrying bags, notebooks and film cameras—followed Gardner out from the surrounding forest.

"The studio's got a lot invested in you," Gardner said, lighting a cigarette. "*I've* got a lot invested in you. We couldn't just let you walk away from it all."

Dock's gaze dropped the ground, shaking his head in disbelief. It was a struggle just to breathe. "I don't... I don't understand... This is about the film?"

Gardner chuckled as he clapped Dock on the shoulder. "Dock, buddy, this *is* the film!"

"What? No. What about Tom Tyler? He was... I... This doesn't make any sense."

Gardner shrugged and kneeled down in front of Dock. "They'll probably use Tommy for the wide shots. Maybe some B-role. You know it was you who gave me the idea, really. Why make a movie about you on some *fictional* adventure, when we could film a real one? The first *real* adventure for America's first *real* hero," he said with a dramatic wave of his hand, as if there was a neon billboard shining above them.

"I'm not a hero," Dock whispered. He glanced over to Tilston and Donovan, both keeping their eyes shamefully to the ground, the former looking almost heartbroken, while a couple of nurses—or more likely make-up artists—cleaned up Donovan's face.

Gardner eyed Dock as he took a drag of cigarette. "What did I tell you? There're no such things as heroes, just people doing what's right by them at the right time for someone else. But that's not really true, is it? When you told me you weren't a 'pulp hero' it got me thinking. Most normal people, if they were offered in on Rothstein's scam, they would've taken it in a second. Hell with your talent, you coulda played the game any way you wanted and made ten times what you're worth now. But no, you went on the straight and narrow. And then that shoot out. Dock, you have any idea what kinda man it takes to single handedly fight off a mob's hit squad? All the things you've done, everything you've seen— Like it or not Doyle, you are the world's first, living breathing pulp hero."

"You sick son of a bitch," Dock cursed, his shock making way for a boiling rage. "The people I... *killed*..."

Gardner waved this away. "We're insured, don't worry about it. Besides they were locals so who the fuck cares? Not me, I'll be honest. We hired 'em about a month ago. You know, they were speaking Spanish this whole time? You'd think you and I've been down to Mexico so many goddamn times one of us would have picked up some of it, but it's all Greek to me." He leaned forward and lowered his voice. "Also, some advice, if you don't want people knowing who you really are, you probably shouldn't keep all your secrets in a tin box on top of your armoire. I found that thing three years ago *just sitting there.*"

"Jimmy, we're gonna need to do some pick-ups on this one," Witney called from the other side of the clearing.

"Get Tommy out of his trailer and see if we can match the shots," Gardner shouted back as he got back to his feet. "Directors. They're are so needy," he murmured to Dock. "On the plane down he kept yammering on and on about this shot and that shot. And that was a *direct* flight here, only one stop over up in—hell, I don't remember the name. I swear if he wasn't so damn talented I would've killed him."

"What's stopping me from killing you?" Dock growled as he stood up.

"Come on, Dock," Gardner snorted, placing his cigarette between his lips. "I know you better than that."

His face blood-red, Dock raised his pistol to Gardner's head. All around them the crew fell silent. "Tell me I won't."

Gardner stumbled back a step, his eyes never leaving the gun barrel. "This isn't funny, Dock," his voice beginning to quaver.

"I've killed seven people. What's one more?"

"Come on… Don't be stupid."

"You thought I was," Dock snarled, pressing the barrel up against Gardner's forehead. No one dared moved closer. "You thought you knew me. You don't. *No one does.*"

A tear streamed down Gardner's cheek. "Dock… Please."

Dock pulled back the hammer.

Gardner fell to his knees, the crotch of his pants growing dark as urine spilled down his leg. Sobbing, he closed his eyes, unable to face the darkness. "Dock, don't do this!"

Dock pressed the revolver harder against Gardner's skull. The seconds passed slowly, the only sound the quiet rustle of the leaves in the wind, the silence threatening to break with the sound of a gunshot. Dock could feel everyone's eyes upon him, watching in horror as their national hero proved to be nothing more than a petty thug. Maybe that's what they wanted, to celebrate a hero born in blood.

He was going to show them he was more than that.

"You're not worth the bullet," Dock growled as he holstered his gun and turned away. He kicked aside the narrow opening to the cage and dragged Harold out and removed his false bindings.

Gardner gasped in relief before letting out a small cough, droplets of blood flecking his chin. He gazed down at the arrowhead sticking out from his chest. "Hell," he softly croaked before silently toppling over.

"Oh no," Tilston whispered, realizing instantly what was about to begin.

Dock spun around, gaping at Gardner's body in shock as the sky darkened with a storm of arrows.

The shrieks were sudden and deafening, the sound of arrows piercing flesh like popcorn on a stove. Blood splattered everywhere, misting into the air. An arrow struck Nathaniel in the stomach. The screenwriter dropped to his knees, gripping the arrow as though he were trying to keep it in place. Two struck Whitney in the head and neck; he was dead before he hit the ground. Several arrows sliced at Dock as he and Harold slid up against the cage, temporarily sheltered from the onslaught. As the last of the arrows hit the ground painted men began to pour out from the trees, their stone blades making work of the survivors.

"This is not happening!" Harold screeched, watching the slaughter. "This can't be happening! What are we going to do?"

Dock grabbed Harold by the arm. "Run," he whispered, pulling them into the brush.

•••

The trees were a blur as Dock and Harold raced towards the coast. Beneath the rush of motion Dock thought he could hear the natives moving through the brush, closing in around them. He tightened his grip on his revolver, finding little comfort in its weight. They were outnumbered ten-to-one, if not more. No matter how many bullets he had, it wouldn't be enough; so they ran until their muscles began to quiver and their lungs threatened to collapse. Caked in sweat and dirt, they pushed themselves forward, fighting exhaustion while vigilantly eying the trees around them.

"You still remember how to kill?" Harold quietly asked, nervously watching the shadows. "Or has being the 'Lincoln of Baseball' made you soft."

"You didn't hear about the shootout with Rothstein in Chicago?" Dock whispered.

"So you really did kill 'the Brain.' And here I thought it was just an urban legend," Harold scoffed.

"Where do you think I got this limp? Sometimes there's truth to legends."

"Or sometimes they're just *lies*," Harold spit back. "'Dock Doyle,' what kinda *name* is that?"

Dock pushed aside a branch with the muzzle of his gun and eyed the path ahead. "You remember the job we did in the Navy Yards?"

Harold furrowed his brow in thought. "When we took out Benjamin?" he asked after a moment.

Dock nodded as he stepped forward. "There was a boat pulling in. Big damn thing; almost thought it was the *Titanic*. The foghorn blew as it approached the pier and I overheard one of the longshoremen yell that he needed help to 'dock *Doyle*,'" he said, and added with a shrug: "Thought it sounded good."

"Huh," Harold noised. "Kinda like Mark Twain."

Eyebrow raised, Dock glanced back at his brother. "I didn't know you could read."

"It's been twenty years," Harold said defiantly. "A lot's changed."

"I've noticed," Dock observed, tapping his scalp.

Harold grimaced. "We can't all have ma's hair, David."

"Shame, isn't it?" Dock commented, unable to hide the satisfied grin on his face.

Several minutes passed as they pushed further into the jungle. The sun was getting lower in the sky. It would be night soon. Dock confessed to himself he had little sense if they were moving in the right direction or if they were just going around in circles, but better to keep moving, keep going forward. Don't look back. Die running, not waiting.

"He regretted it, you know," Harold said a while later, his voice throaty and strained. "Making you leave like that. Don't think he ever forgave himself."

Dock stopped short, hearing something rustle in the woods; too big to be an animal. He looked to Harold and pressed a finger to his lips. "Doesn't mean I have to forgive him," he said aloud, tapping his ear.

Harold nodded in understanding. "He would ask about you. Especially towards the end."

Dock raised his gun and inched over towards the source of the sound. "Did he ask why his 'Goliath' became a baseball player?"

"He never listened to the radio or read the papers, and Lord help him if he ever paid attention to baseball—" Harold said with a laugh. "He never knew *who* you became. I wanted to tell him, but ma, you know how she was, she didn't want me to say nothing."

"Good," Dock said, holstering his gun.

Harold's eyes went wide, an expression that screamed "What are you doing!?" Aloud he calmly said: "He would've been proud."

"No, he wouldn't have," Dock growled before he violently reached into the bushes and pulled out Tilston and Donovan, and tossed them to the ground.

"Mr. Doyle! Please don't shoot," Tilston begged, holding his hands high as Dock pulled his revolver.

"You don't get to make requests," Dock snarled, pressing the muzzle of the gun into Tilston's stomach. "Tell me why I shouldn't kill you both now?"

"Please, Mr. Doyle!" Tilston pleaded. "We had no idea it was going to be like this, you have to believe us. We're just actors! The studio hired us so they could film this… *adventure*. Had we known, we would have never…"

Dock scowled, but took his finger off the trigger. "Tilston your real name?"

The man nodded. "Yes. But I'm not a Doctor," he said, his British accent gone. "Hell, I barely finished college. They brought me on 'cause I could speak Spanish and looked intelligent.'"

Dock turned to Donovan. "What about you?"

"I was supposed to be your love interest," she whispered, her English accent gone, never daring to look directly at Dock. "That's why I—"

"Lady Donna Donovan your *real* name, too?"

She shook her head. "Mattie. Mattie Whipple. 'Donna Donovan' was a play on the 'double d.' Dock Doyle, Donna Donovan. They thought it sounded good."

Their clothing was torn, cuts and bruises lining their arms and exhausted faces. More than anything Dock could see the pure, unbridled fear in their eyes; the same kind of fear he had seen in Rachel's eyes before—

"How's your hearing?" Dock asked calmly as he helped Mattie to her feet. His stomach turned at the sight of the subtle handprint on her cheek, his eyes fell to his feet.

"Better," she quietly replied, unconsciously touching her ear. "Still ringing."

Dock turned to Tilston. "Were you followed?"

"I don't know—" he admitted. "When they attacked, Mattie and I— We just ran. There were others but— It was dumb luck that we found you."

"Our 'co-stars' seemed a little angry," Dock commented.

"Can you blame them?" Tilston asked. He wiped the sweat from his brow, smudging dirt across his face. "Gardner probably promised them gold and diamonds."

"I guess getting killed wasn't in the contract," Harold said with a morbid smirk.

Dock ignored his brother's comment and looked up to the darkening sky. "We should keep moving," he said. "Can you get us back to the boat, Tilston?"

Tilston nodded. "It'll be harder without the sun, but I can get us there."

"Then we should get moving," Dock said. He wrapped an arm around Mattie and bore some of her weight, then to the group, he said: "Keep your eyes open. This is *their* land, for all we know they could be anywhere. Stick together, stay close and we might just get out of this alive."

And together they went out into the darkness.

•••

"I want you to really consider what you're doing," Rachel said, her pale blue eyes driving into his; their fingers intertwined. She was leaning over the railings, strands of her hair fluttered in the cold Chicago wind, the lights giving her a faint aura. He swore he had never seen her look this beautiful.

"I have," he reassured her with a smile and squeeze of her hand.

She raised an eyebrow. "Have you?"

"Sweetheart."

She shrugged and held her hands up defensively. "Doesn't hurt to check. I don't want you getting cold feet or anything. This is a big step for both of us."

"Big step for me, you mean."

"No, I mean big step for us," she retorted. "This isn't exactly a cakewalk for me, you know."

He gave her a small, guilty nod. "I know."

"But know that no matter what happens, you know I'll always love you, Davi—"

"Dock," he corrected.

Rachel winced in embarrassment. "Dock, right. Sorry. But you can't really blame me if I want to use the name of the man I fell in love with."

"That man doesn't exist anymore," Dock whispered.

"Coulda' fooled me," she said, tapping him in the shoulder.

"Doyle! Dock Doyle!" a man with a clipboard hollered from across the field; his White Sox uniform dusty and faded. The other coaches and managers were milling about as the latest try-out tossed away his bat, dejected; and somewhere in the stands Comiskey was watching it all. "I said: Dock Doyle!" the man yelled again, his patience wearing thin.

"That's me," Dock said, lifting up his bat, hoping his face didn't betray his nervousness. This was only a baseball try-out, he tried to remind himself, it wasn't like he was about to have a gunfight with a rival gang.

"Is it?" Rachel asked with a half-grin.

"Shush." He leaned his forehead against hers. "Wish me luck."

Rachel kissed him on the lips, sending shivers down his spine even now. "You don't need luck," she whispered.

"Why's that?"

"Cause you're my hero."

•••

"Look at you, David, acting the hero; protecting the damsel-in-distress," Harold whispered to Dock awhile later. Mattie was several feet ahead alongside Tilston, her hand holding his; it wasn't a grip of love, not in the romantic sense, at least; it was one of protection, like the love of a sister for an older brother. It left a bitter taste in Dock's mouth.

"Nothing heroic about it. Tilston can get us back to the boat, that'll get us home. Just doing what's right by me and it happens to sound good to everyone else."

Harold shook his head in disbelief. "It's funny, y'know. After everything, between the two of us, *you* ended up being the biggest bullshit artist in the world. Do these people know who you are? Who Dock Doyle *really* is?"

Dock firmed his lips but remained silent.

"Heh," Harold chuckled, knowing he had gotten under his brother's skin. He thrust his chin at the actors ahead of them. "You think they would look at you the same way? Do you think *America* would still consider you its favorite son if they knew you were an enforcer for the mob? Not even that, do they know you were a *Jewish* gangster? The 'Lincoln of Baseball,' a *kike* and a killer. The press would eat it up, wouldn't they? Woo! That would be the day, wouldn't it? How much you think they'd offer me to talk? A million? Two? Hell, I agreed to work with your buddy Jimmy for three thousand."

Dock stopped and looked at Harold in muted shock. "Is that why you got involved in this? Three thousand dollars?"

"Business went to shit a few years ago what with the Depression and all. After dad died the whole organization started to fall apart. By the time your friend Jimmy stopped by it was just me, a gun and a glass of a whiskey."

Dock grabbed a tree branch to steady himself.

"Hey, look, I could've gone to the press years ago," Harold confessed as he gripped Dock's shoulder. "I would've been set for life, but I didn't. That must count for *something.*"

Dock kept his gaze on the ground, unable to look his brother in the eye. "Not much," he said with venom.

Harold watched him turn away. Scratching the back of his neck he asked: "Why *didn't* you just leave me there?"

"Because," Dock replied without looking back, "you're all I have left."

"We're almost there!" Tilston called back, grinning. "Just over this ridge and we should see the boat—" He climbed and peered over the embankment where his smile instantly faded. "Shit."

•••

Dock inched forward on his stomach, risking only a quick view of the shoreline before ducking back behind the ridge, his heart racing. The beach was overrun with natives, slinging arrows at the boat in a vain attempt to sink it. Even though Dock knew the natives wouldn't succeed, he still needed to figure out how to get himself and the others onto the boat. There was a narrow chain of rocks, curving out from the shore, ending only a few feet shy of the boat's anchor. They could walk over the rocks and swim out to the anchor and climb up there, but they would still need to get past the horde of natives.

"How many of them are there?" Harold asked.

Dock pressed his lips together and shook his head in defeat. "More than we can handle."

"Sitting around isn't exactly an option, either."

"I know, I know," Dock murmured, running a hand through his hair. "Just let me think for a second."

"Come on, you killed Rothstein and a dozen of his men, this should be nothing!"

"And I got Rachel killed!" Dock nearly screamed, his eyes red, fighting back tears. "I don't want any more people dying because of me!" As he said that, the idea, at once brilliant and foolish, popped into his mind. He ran his hand over his face, weighing the options again before coming to the same conclusion. There were six bullets in his revolver, the stone blade and his fists. Not enough to save the day, but just enough to put up a fight.

He looked at Tilston, Mattie and Harold, their faces dirty, bloody and full of fear. They didn't deserve this, least of all Harold, but if any of them were to make it home, this was the *only* option.

And in the end, all he really had left was his baby brother.

"Goddammit—" he sighed. "Harold, you see those rocks? Remember when we used to go to Coney Island back in the day?"

Harold peered out. "Yeah, but how are we going to make sure they don't see—" His jaw fell open in realization. "Shit, you're not telling me—"

"You'll have to swim over and climb up the anchor. Tilston, if En and the others are missing, you think you can get the engines started?"

"I think so," Tilston said with a hesitant nod.

"What about you?" Harold asked, already knowing the answer.

Dock met his brother's gaze. "I'll buy you time. Can't say how much, hopefully it'll be enough."

"Mr. Doyle—" Mattie took a half step forward, tentatively holding out her hand as if to touch him. "You can't be serious."

"Don't worry," he said with a sardonic grin. "Once you make it back you'll all be *celebrities*. They'll be clamoring to hear you tell your stories. You thought three thousand was a lot of money? Just you wait. And the studios? They'll probably make a movie about all this. Ain't that grand?"

"David, don't be insane!" Harold sobbed, tears welling up in his eyes.

"Don't try and talk me out of this, Harold," he said, firmly grasping his brother's shoulder. His smile broadened but his voice threatened to crack, the failing bravado of man who had accepted his fate. "I've made my decision. I came here to rescue you, might as well live up to that." He looked to Tilston and Mattie. "Stay low, move quick. The rocks will be slippery, and climbing up the anchor won't be easy, so be careful."

"You're a better man than the one dad raised you to be," Harold croaked, the first of many tears streaming down his cheek.

Dock allowed himself a quiet laugh. "Yeah… I'm surprised too."

•••

Dock was ready now.

He moved through the brush until he was directly behind the crowd of natives. Harold and the others were going to wait until his signal before they risked climbing down the ridge. Dock would keep the natives busy as long as he could, but it was up to them to get to the boat before it was too late.

Dock Doyle closed his eyes and tilted his face up to the sky. He remembered back to the day before everything had gone wrong, before Chick Gandil tried to bring him in on the fix. His two-run homer had given the Sox the game, but it wasn't the roar of the crowd he heard, nor was it the rush of rounding the bases he recalled.

It was the smile on Rachel's face, sitting in the sidelines with Richie, his little boy, not even a year-old, giggling with delight.

That was all he had ever been fighting for: a way home. Maybe now, finally—

David Dauer opened his eyes and rushed forward, firing into the crowd, taking down two, three, four natives before they began to charge towards him, unleashing a storm of arrows. Pain exploded in his body as arrows flew into his shoulder and side. One arrow sliced across his hand, knocking his gun free, another hit him in his wounded leg, awakening a rage within him. He drew the stone blade and began slicing through anyone that came in his way. He kept pushing forward, kept fighting without mercy and without pleasure. All that mattered was that he stayed standing long enough for the others. Stay standing long enough so the others could live. Stay standing. Just stay standing.

An arrow struck him in the chest, piercing his lung. As blood welled up in his throat, he thought he heard the boat's engines start up… but maybe it was only Doctor Dread's machine.

A weak smile pulled at his lips and David Dauer kept standing.

The End

The Fact and Fiction of David Dauer

Allow me to leave some room for debate.

Dock Doyle is an examination of the "hero," how we perceive them through the veil of fiction and ideals, contrasted by who they really are. In a world much like our own, circumstances pushed a man from obscurity into the spotlight, becoming the world's first, living pulp hero.

Real heroes portraying themselves in films is not a new idea. Historical figures such as Houdini starred in silent films such as *The Master of Mystery*, *The Man from Beyond* and *The Grim Game*, which blurred the lines of reality and fiction. *The Great Game*, in particular, featured an aerial stunt in which two biplanes accidentally collided, with Houdini's stunt man dangling on a rope from one of the planes. The advertisements went so far as to claim the stuntman was Houdini himself, further obscuring the boundary between the real Houdini and his fictional adventures.

Then there are the contemporary dime novel stories of Wild Bill Hickok, Buffalo Bill, and Jesse James, amongst others. These stories were, more often than not, exaggerated or wholly fictional tales invented either by the subjects or writers, reaching the point that it is now difficult to distinguish between history and fabrication. The line is further blurred as their legends grow over time, taking on a mythical quality, gradually turning these flawed, imperfect men into idealized heroes.

The distinction between fact and fiction was often muddled in the other direction. According to Jim Harmon and Donald F. Glut's *The Great Movie Serials: Their Sound and Fury*, Kirk Alyn went uncredited in the first Superman serial, the studio's advertising claiming that it had "hired Superman himself" and that Kirk Alyn was only playing Clark Kent.

Even today, with the constant torrent of media drowning us with heavily edited reality TV, mockumentaries and news channels that twist facts, what is and what isn't becomes a subject of debate rather than a simple question of "yes" or "no." Biographical films turn historical events into dramatized moments, changing events so that the story has a more satisfying conclusion.

Fiction is reality and fact is imaginary.

Pulp heroes are a fiction, an ideal, meant, in part, to inspire the reader to become something more than what they are. Characters like Doc Savage were created to typify everything great about what we *could* be; "Christliness," as Dent put it; a conceit encapsulated in Doc's mantra: "Let me strive every moment of my life to make myself better and better, to the best of my ability, that all may profit by it…" It is an admirable concept.

But we do not live in an ideal world, and as much as we would like to see the world painted in blacks and whites, we exist eternally in a world of gray. There have been heroes and there have been monsters, but more often than not the tides of history are pushed and pulled by complex individuals that are not so easily defined. Lincoln saved the Union but suspended civil liberties; Hitler killed millions but was a vegetarian. In this muddy world of flawed, imperfect people, could we ever, truly have a pulp hero? And if we did, would he—could he—truly be that ideal? Or would he be flawed and imperfect—*human*—just like the rest of us?

Is Dock Doyle, the ideal pulp hero, any different than David Dauer, the flawed, imperfect man? Or rather is it the expectations we place on one, and not the other, that define our perception of them? Dock Doyle is an idyllic testament to morality in the face of corruption. But while his name was plastered across billboards, bubble gum wrappers and pulp magazines, was he really the "Lincoln of Baseball?" Was it Dock Doyle who gave up everything for love, who got out of the car to face the mobsters, who lost everything he held sacred in this world?

Dock Doyle is a name, a fiction, a manufactured escape, at first for an individual and then for a country. What truly made the hero, what drove him forward was the man—flawed and imperfect—David Dauer.

•••

Adam Lance Garcia - Growing up in Brooklyn, New York in the late 1980s, Adam was raised on comic books and movie serials. His first novella, "Green Lama: Horror in Clay," was nominated for Best Short Story in the 2009 Pulp Factory Awards. His first novel Green Lama: Unbound won the 2010 Pulp Factory Awards for Best Novel of the Year and Best Interior Art for the work of his frequent collaborator, Mike Fyles; as well as the 2010 Pulp Ark Award for Best Pulp Revival.

His short story "Green Lama & the Case of the Final Column" will be featured in the Altus Press reprints of the original pulp stories; and his audio-play "Green Lama & the Curse of Liberty Island" will be produced and released by AudioComics as part of their "Pulp Adventures" series.

He is currently at work on his next novel, *Green Lama: Crimson Circle* as well as several other original projects, including a Dock Doyle anthology.

A MAN CALLED MONGREL
"Just Another Day at the Office"

By Derrick Ferguson

Manhattan, New York
The Chrysler Building, 52nd Floor

Angelika Peary stuck her head out of her office and bawled into the sudden quiet of the office suite; "Has anybody got the TV in the conference room turned on yet? I'm on the phone with CNN!"

Somebody hollered back in the affirmative that she should come join them as yes; the program was just about to start. Angelika nodded to herself and continued her conversation.

"Yes, Mr. Kierzewski, I assure you that Mr. Henderson will be available for Piers Morgan next week…. yes, I know he's broken the last two interview dates but you surely must be aware that Mr. Henderson is an extraordinarily busy man. His recent acceptance of the position of Executive Security Consultant for Alternative Technologies covers an incredibly broad latitude of duties and responsibilities which can demand his attention at any time of the day or night…. yes, yes…well, we'll just have to pray for the best and hope nothing comes up that will force us to postpone the interview yet again. Please convey my most sincere apologies to Mr. Morgan… thank you again, Mr. Kierzewski…. yes, I'll be in touch…. have a good one."

Angelika clicked off her talk stick and let it dangle from the silver chain hanging around her neck as she closed her office door and strode rapidly down the long corridor on her brand new $800 Else Pauza high heels to the main conference room where her 28 person staff sat around the long rectangular mahogany table which was polished every day to a gleam so bright it was almost as if the table was somehow lit from within. Cardboard cups of piping hot coffee, bottles of water and fruit juices were being passed around by an intern as she entered. The large square smartglass picture windows had been darkened so as to cut down on the glare from the bright late morning sun but even the darkened view of the Manhattan skyline was awesomely breathtaking.

Angelika took her seat at the head of the table, straightening the jacket of her metallic peach business suit with a firm two-handed tug. "How's it going so far?" she asked, gesturing with her chin at the far wall, which was actually one huge LCD screen.

Nikki Hagar, her lanky, brunette secretary gave her boss thumbs up. "So far, so good. I only hope that Mr. Henderson gets there before the fireworks start. You sure we shouldn't alert the complex security?"

Angelika shook her head. "Mr. Henderson was very explicit about that. He said he'd catch up to them before they hit South Carolina. And if he doesn't—"

Angelika didn't finish the sentence. She didn't have to. This day could turn out to

109

be a disaster in much more than public relations terms. It could also end in death. Angelika took in a deep breath and sat back in her high backed leather chair, folding her arms under her breasts. Nothing to do at this end but wait and see what happened. She turned her attention to the screen. The TV was tuned into *ATI*, the news and information channel owned and operated 24/7/365 by Alternative Technologies. Designed to keep the public abreast of the activities and accomplishments of Alternative Technologies, today it was broadcasting the Opening Day Ceremonies of Alternative Technologies. Angelika only hoped it didn't end in blood.

•••

South Carolina
The Henderson Institute of Alternative Technologies

❝   and now we continue with our exclusive coverage of the Opening Day •••Ceremonies of Alternative Technologies hosted by our own Dr. Zita Laranjo. Zita?"

An extraordinarily beautiful woman appeared on the screen, dressed smartly in a conservative sky blue business outfit. Although it was obvious that the woman tried to downplay the remarkable physical beauty of her body in the choice of her clothing, even Stevie Wonder could not fail to see that she was well endowed in all the places a woman should be endowed. She looked more like a Victoria Secret's model than the holder of advanced degrees in Mathematical Arts, Industrial Physics and Artificial Intelligence Ethical Instruction. One had the impression that the rectangular frame glasses she wore were a prop to help her look more scholarly but they only drew attention to her lovely, almond shaped light gray eyes. Even on a television screen her remarkably exotic looks were quite apparent and among her male co-workers there was a secret pool as to what mix of ethnic backgrounds could have produced such a strikingly beautiful woman. It was highly doubtful that they would ever accurately pinpoint her Danish/Hawaiian heritage.

"Thank you, Warren. It's a beautiful day here in South Carolina where it's a comfortable 60 degrees under sunny skies without a cloud in sight and we're only a few minutes away from Dr. Sylvester Henderson's dedication speech which will climax with him throwing a switch that will symbolically turn on the power here at the new site of Alternative Technologies."

"Now what do you mean by 'symbolically', Zita?"

"Warren, the place has been actively working for close to sixteen months now so of course it has power, but today is a special day here as the complex will, for the first time, be 100% up and running. It's a very big day for not only Dr. Henderson but his wife, his mother and his father, all of whom are respected scientists in their fields. Alternative Technologies was previously scattered in separate facilities all over the country but over the past eight years this central complex facility was constructed and will now serve as the American headquarters for the company, directing their international offices from right here as well as maintaining most of their research and theoretical departments, the developmental and administrative divisions of AT as well."

Dr. Zita Laranjo paused a minute to smile and step slightly to one side, extended her right arm to indicate the sprawl of buildings behind her. It looked like a small city behind her with tall, slim buildings that glittered and sparkled in the midday sun surrounded by smaller but no less impressive structures. "I'll be taking you on a virtual tour of the complex after Dr. Henderson's speech but for right now let me give you facts about the complex. Built on 28,000 acres of land, The Henderson Institute of Alternative Technologies is a residential community in its own right as well as being a scientific one. It has its own zoning restrictions and building codes, its own roads, lakes, hotels, airport, golf courses, night clubs, and theatres as well as providing its own energy, water, police and fire department."

"It's an incredible achievement, Zita."

"It certainly is, Warren, and one that I'm proud to say I've had a hand in. I've been working with Dr. Henderson and his family for close to eleven years now and…" Dr. Zita Laranjo stopped talking, her hand going up to the small earbug plugged firmly into her right ear. "…we're going to go to the podium now where Dr. Henderson is just beginning his speech."

The picture on the screen changed to a podium erected in front of an imposing black slab of a building that thrust upwards some hundred stories. The unseen Zita's voice spoke quietly: "The podium you're seeing is in front of the Main Building of the complex. It houses not only the administrative and executive departments of Alternative Technologies but the Network of Internet Security and Acquisitions, the Data Administrative Committee Headquarters and The Multimedia Development and Networking Division."

"Sounds impressive, Zita," the unseen Warren chimed in, right on cue.

"It is, I assure you. And yes, I can see Dr. Henderson approaching the microphone. On the podium behind him you can see various AT executives and key staffers as well as Dr. Henderson's family. His mother, Dr. Rebecca Henderson. His father, Dr. Nayland Henderson. His wife, Dr. Mirella Henderson and his three children. Daughters Tamara and Toyelle and his son, Tyrell."

"They're not doctors yet, eh, Zita?"

"Not yet, but give it time, Warren. The Henderson children are extraordinarily bright for their ages. Tyrell is only fifteen and already his experiments with Aberrant Polonium Configurations have research scientists old enough to be his grandfather scratching their heads trying to figure out just how he's doing it."

"Doesn't Dr. Henderson also have a brother…"

"I'm afraid that's all the time we have, Warren! Dr. Henderson's going to speak now!"

•••

The thunderous swell of applause exploded from the crowd of hundreds assembled in the circular plaza in front of the main building. Dr. Sylvester Henderson looked extremely trim and athletic in his black business suit, crisp white shirt and red silk tie. His Verdi style beard and mustache looked freshly trimmed. As indeed it was not more than thirty minutes ago. His high forehead and wide bright eyes bespoke of intelligence far above the average. And he was an above average man, having spent years knocking around the world while amassing a tremendous fortune due to his incredible scientific achievements. And he was still a relatively young man with decades of productive research to look forward to. He cleared his throat, stepped closer to the microphone and spoke:

"There are no words adequate enough to express the joy and pride I feel today at having all of you here to share this day with myself, my family and my friends. Alternative Technologies is more than just a scientific research facility. It's a way of life dedicated to finding new and innovative ways to use the ever expanding technological wonders of our age to helping us live better and more fulfilling lives, to living longer with no disease and no pain, to feeding the millions that are still going hungry, to wiping out birth defects and…"

Sylvester Henderson stopped, frowning slightly. He had heard something and soon the crowd heard it as well. It was the muted roaring of powerful jets coming from the north.

The unseen Warren asked; "Zita, can you see what's going on? Dr. Henderson has just stopped his speech and we can't see any reason why. Is everything…"

"There's some sort of aircraft coming in from the north, Warren! Very fast and very low! It could be some sort of attack but I'm not getting anything on the security channel! I…"

Indeed, the one-man aircraft was moving very fast indeed. It looked so stubby and bulbous it hardly seemed capable of getting up off the ground, much less traveling at the speed it which it was going, heading right for the podium. The wings on the sides were elongated triangles and at the rear of the craft were a number of smaller fins flanking six powerful jets glowing red-hot. And in the middle of all this was a half-transparent globe in which a man could be dimly seen. The crowd screamed and broke for cover as the stubby aircraft's jets sparked and dense black smoke poured from the rear of the aircraft.

The canopy popped open and a man leaped from the aircraft, which twisted and zoomed upwards, following the pre-programmed course that the pilot had punched in before bailing out. He landed on the podium as lightly as a lynx, his narrowed eyes sweeping the plaza that was rapidly emptying of people. The stubby aircraft corkscrewed up and away from the complex, trailing a ribbon of smoke as it yowled up into the sky.

He was an easy six feet even, dressed in gleaming black boots and dark blue pants of some denim like material. Over his Olympian musculature he wore a skintight

He landed on the podium as lightly as a lynx,

collarless black shirt and over that a high collared double-breasted brown leather vest. A wide nylon duty belt encircled his waist. An oversized handgun was in a slanted holster between his shoulder blades and on his hands thick gauntlets the same color and material as his vest protected his hands and forearms. He turned his rust colored eyes to scanning the skies as he barked orders: "Get inside now. They're coming. I barely beat them here."

Sylvester did not argue just asked a question: "You see them?"

The big man pointed at three dots in the sky that were rapidly coming closer. "Delegene Mark II flyers, modified for combat, just as my informants told me."

"You sure you can take them?"

"No doubt. Get outta here."

Sylvester began herding the people on the podium toward the main building. His son, Tyrell paused long enough to shout over his shoulder, "Kick their ass, Uncle Mongrel!"

Mongrel smiled slightly and said; "Help your dad get the family to safety, Tyrell. And watch your language." He turned back to watch the tri-engine Vibroflyers come in closer and closer. "Time to go to work," he said, running to the edge of the podium and with a powerful thrust of his legs launched himself into the air right at the flyers.

Mongrel's amazing leap took the three men in the flyer totally by surprise. Despite the fact that he was 6 feet and weighed 190 pounds of solid muscle, he moved as quickly and as smoothly as a Russian gymnast. He went up and over the canopy of the lead flyer, landing right in the center of the large open flight deck. Without a word, without a sound, Mongrel went on the offensive. A devastating backhand fist slammed the pilot's head into the control panel. Metal and bone crunched as fat yellow sparks jumped from the ruined control panel and danced over the instruments. The second man caught a booted foot in his midsection that kicked him out of the flyer to land on the ground with enough bone-jangling force knocking him out immediately. The last man waded in, desperately throwing a punch that Mongrel easily slipped as he simply picked up the man bodily and heaved him out of the flyer.

Mongrel grabbed up the pilot, tucked him under his arm and jumped from the flyer, which tilted crazily on its side due the sudden and abrupt shift in weight loss. It landed on edge and rolled along like a child's hoop, the engines crunching under its own weight. The flyer continued rolling for maybe eighty feet before finally crashing into a fountain. It tipped over, smashed to the ground and lay at rest, smoking and crackling from the fire in the engine pods.

The second flyer came in low, seeking to ram Mongrel who dived to the ground and as the flyer zoomed overhead, he rolled over and drew from the holster between his shoulder blades something that looked a lot like a oversized .357 Magnum revolver but was much more. Developed by Mongrel's longtime acquaintance, Josef Bianchin, one of the ten best ballistic experts in the world, the Bianchin Omnipurpose Pistol, or BOP Gun as Mongrel affectionately liked to call it, didn't fire conventional bullets. Each and every shell had a separate and specialized purpose. And right now he fired the high explosive shell right up through the bottom of the flyer.

Mongrel himself had flown this type of flyer a lot some nine years ago when fighting in a small war on the Ricia Peninsula in Greece and a crucial weakness had been revealed to him the hard way in regard to a design flaw in the Delegene Mark II flyer. One that he was now more than happy to share with the three gentlemen in this craft: the fuel tanks were on the bottom, which was the most vulnerable part of the craft.

The flyer exploded, cascading ribbons of blazing fuel all over the plaza as the craft crashed to the ground in a smoking heap of black, twisted metal. The three men ran around, their flight suits on fire, beating at themselves in a futile effort to put out the rapidly spreading flames.

Mongrel stood up, twirled his BOP Gun back into the holster. "Dummies," he muttered to himself. "Didn't they learn how to stop, drop and roll in elementary school?" He noticed movement out of the corner of his eye. The pilot of the first flyer feebly tried to crawl away. "C'mere, you." Mongrel picked him up as if the man weighed no more than a napkin and held him effortlessly up in the air with one hand. "And where do you think *you're* sneaking off to?"

"Release me! Or the others will attack and slay you!"

"I don't think so." Mongrel twisted him around so that the pilot could watch the third flyer's south end as it headed quickly north. "They saw you go down so they saw it was time to cut out. You're on your own, cuddles. Just me and you. And while I know some of what you planned, I don't know it all and you're gonna tell me."

"I will tell you nothing! Do you hear me? NOTHING!"

"That'll change," Mongrel promised him. Security officers rapidly encircled Mongrel and the attackers, using fire extinguishers to put out the fires. The shrill wail of sirens could be heard approaching. Dressed in trim, tight fitting uniforms of black trimmed with gold and green, all colors of Alternative Technologies, they approached Mongrel warily, handguns drawn. "Okay, mister. Just put him down and take a step back. Put your hands on your head."

•••

Mongrel sighed. "I don't suppose any of you recognize me from my lectures, seminars and training exercises I've given here on security procedures over the last eight months? Look close."

"Mr. Henderson?!"

"Bingo. Didn't think I'd be so hard to recognize. Here, take charge of this lump." Mongrel tossed the pilot into the waiting arms of a pair of security officers. The others crowded around Mongrel.

"Well, sir, we've only seen you in suits before. That getup you're wearing…can't blame us for not looking at your face."

"I hear you but I can't exactly pull off the stuff I just did wearing a three piece Armani, now can I?" Mongrel joined in the good-natured laughing of the security officers and he gently pushed past them and headed for the main building, tossing orders over his shoulders. "Get maintenance on cleaning up the plaza and get those men who need medical attention over to the hospital. I'm going to check on my family and then I'll want to interrogate those men personally."

•••

Manhattan, New York
The Chrysler Building, 43rd Floor

Angelika Peary clapped her hands sharply, catching everybody's attention. "Okay, people, man your desks. That was just seen worldwide and in a few minutes we're going to be working like government mules, so hop on it."

The staffers filed out of the conference room and into the main office area where everyone had their own desks, no cubicles. Neat gleaming bronze nameplates were given a last polish and pens, papers, computer flat screens were adjusted. The staffers took their seats and waited expectantly.

And as if on cue, every phone in the place began ringing. The staffers snatched them up, answering in easy, confident voices; "Henderson Executive Security Consultations. How may we help you?"

A grinning Angelika watched the sudden wave of activity in the office as her secretary came over to stand next to her. Nikki Hagar just shook her head in amazement. "I still can't believe that you pulled it off. How'd you ever get Mr. Henderson to lend his name out to the company?"

Angelika motioned for Nikki to follow her back to her office as she answered. "It wasn't all that hard. Mongrel and I have known each other for a long time, back when I was a Secret Service agent. We've worked together a couple of times and when I heard about him going to work for his brother I knew it could be a gold mine if I played it right. We get his name and the use of his services on the high profile assignments and for publicity. I handle the rest. I predict it's going to be a very lucrative and rewarding working relationship all the way around."

Angelika's talk stick booped for attention. She clicked it on and put it to her ear. "Angelika Peary…well, hello, Mr. Combs! Good to hear from you again…"

•••

South Carolina, United States of America
Henderson Institute of Alternative Technologies

"I'm not interested in what reasons you had, Sylvester! It was damned irresponsible of you to take such chances with not only your lives but ours as well!"

Despite being only five feet five inches tall, when Rebecca Henderson got her mad on she could appear to dwarf everybody else in the room and that included the son who towered over her. He spoke softly, quietly, "Mother..."

"And don't you dare 'Mother' me! If you knew there was a threat on your life, why in God's name didn't you take the appropriate measures?"

"But I did, Mother. I informed Mongrel and he investigated..."

"Somebody mention my name?" The door of the library opened and Mongrel stepped in. The top ten floors of the Main Building were for the exclusive use of The Henderson family and their personal staff. Comprised of offices, laboratories, libraries, studies, conference rooms as well as playrooms and bedrooms, Sylvester had brought everybody up there to wait for word from his brother. Mongrel crossed the spacious room in several long strides to embrace Sylvester warmly.

"You okay, Mongrel?" Sylvester stepped back, looked his brother up and down. "Not even a scratch."

Mongrel snorted in derision. "Those guys couldn't have taken the kids. Where are they, by the way?"

"They're with their mother. She thought it was best if we talk without them around since we don't know how bad the situation is." Sylvester gestured toward their mother and father. "Mother and Father are understandably upset about our course of action."

"Upset is not the word!" Rebecca snapped, her small bright eyes flashing wrathful fire. "Charalambides, come over here by me, boy!"

"Ma..."

"Don't 'Ma' me! Mind what I say!"

Mongrel reluctantly slouched over to where his mother stood. His father, Nayland Henderson sat cross-legged on a low leather couch, unlit pipe firmly in his teeth, which showed in a wide grin. It never failed to tickle him how his rough and tumble son, famous for adventuring in all the wild corners of the world, respected and feared as a outstandingly dangerous man could suddenly be turned into a little boy at the merest word from his mother. As he drew closer, Rebecca drove a small hard fist into his stomach. Out of respect for his mother, Mongrel doubled up, pretending that it hurt. "Ma, don't do that, okay?"

"I ought to take a switch to you, Charalambides!"

"Ma, how many times I gotta ask you to call me Mongrel?"

"I will not! Charalambides is a fine, distinguished name! It was a name your grandfather was proud of. I thought it was a name you would be proud of as well."

"I *am* proud of it. But Mongrel doesn't take half the day to say."

"Don't change the subject! Why did you let your brother go out there exposed when you knew there were men coming to kill him?"

Mongrel jerked a thumb over a brawny shoulder. "Ask him. I recommended we call off the ceremony but he insisted on going through with it."

Rebecca turned her basilisk gaze on Sylvester. "Is this true, son?"

"It is, Mother." Sylvester held up a hand to indicate he be allowed to finish before Rebecca went into yet another tirade. "You all know how important this day is. I was not about to let anyone or anything ruin it. Mongrel assured me that he could intercept the assassins before they got here." Sylvester smiled at Mongrel. "And if I can't trust my brother's word then who can I trust?"

"You were a tad late, weren't you son?" Nayland asked quietly.

Mongrel nodded, spreading his hands apologetically as he explained; "I followed them from Virginia and was going to take them in North Carolina. I developed engine trouble and by the time the self-repair programs kicked in and corrected the problem, they had gained a lot of ground on me. I damn near burned out the engines catching up to them."

"I still say you should have told us!" Rebecca insisted.

"Enough, woman." Nayland said. He had let her blow off more than enough steam and it was time to rein her in or she'd be going off for the rest of the day. "I can't say I'm entirely pleased with the way the boys handled it and I'd have liked to be told myself. But this isn't the first time we've been in a dangerous spot." Indeed it was not. In their youth, Nayland and Rebecca had done their share of dangerous duty in the service of their country. Nayland pointed the stem of his pipe at his sons. "Don't do that again, boys. Your mother and I stand firmly behind whatever it is you do but we want to be told. Is that understood?"

"Yes, Father."

"Yes, Dad."

"Then we'll speak no more of it." Nayland replaced his pipe and recrossed his legs. "Charalambides, did you find out who those men are and why they're after Sylvester?"

"They're common mercenaries, hired over The DarkNet. Nothing special about them except the flyers they were using. Those don't come cheap. But I had a little 'talk' with the pilot. He'll walk funny for a few days but he'll be okay. And he told me who hired them." Mongrel fixed Sylvester with a curious look. "He said something really strange, Sly. He claims that they were hired by the Spiteri family."

"The Spiteri family?" Nayland asked. "Name's familiar somehow."

"It should be," Mongrel ticked off his fingers as he explained. "Shipping. Munitions. Plasma Energy Plants. Communications. Tellurium Transmuta-tion Technology."

"Ah." Nayland nodded. "*That* Spiteri family."

"If I say so myself, they're easily as influential and wealthy as we are. But I can't think of a reason why they would hire somebody to kill Sly." Mongrel turned back to Sylvester, who looked around for a chair as if in a daze. He slowly sat down on a leather couch, his movements that of a much older, wearier man. Mongrel was at his brother's side in a heartbeat, kneeling down and placing a hand on his knee. "Sylvester? You do know why they want to kill you, don't you?"

Sylvester looked up at Mongrel with eyes that were the color of cold dead ashes. "Dear God, I do know. And they've got a good reason."

"What possible reason could they have for wanting to kill you, man?"

"Because I've killed them, Mongrel. Because of me, the Spiteri family is dead."

•••

Louisiana, United States of America
The Spiteri Family Estate located on The Atchafalaya Basin

The interior of The Bumblebee was illuminated by the many holographic readouts projected onto the clear upper half of the aircraft. Mongrel intently studied the blueprints of the Spiteri family home as well as the security systems specifications as he sat inside the aircraft, sipping from a Thermos that contained a concentrated protein shake of his own concoction. The cold drink went easily down his throat as he planned his strategy. He landed maybe half a mile from the estate and discarded a variety of approaches. He could have contacted the local authorities and asked for an official police escort to go with him. Or he could have called the Spiteri family before hand and asked for a meeting. Mongrel even had the name of the legal firm that handled their affairs. He could have contacted them. Neither method appealed to Mongrel. He much rather use the bold approach: just walk right in, take them by surprise and see who squealed the loudest.

•••

He opened up the upper half of The Bumblebee and climbed out. The air was horribly heavy with humidity but Mongrel ignored it, taking stock of the weapons neatly racked in a small locker behind the pilot's chair. He kept The BOP Gun as he had gotten so used to carrying the versatile weapon that fired a variety of specially designed cartridges. He closed up The Bumblebee and headed off toward the Spiteri main house at a steady jog that looked deceptively slow but ate up the distance to the estate in a surprisingly short amount of time.

As he jogged, Mongrel guiltily reflected that there was a part of him that actually was delighted that this situation had come up. Of course, he didn't want to see any member of his family get hurt or injured but ever since he had come to work with his brother, there had been far too many briefings, meetings, seminars and presentations. He had known what he was getting into when he took the job and nothing delighted him more than being around the family again. He had been away from them and America for far too long, his nearly manic thirst for excitement and adventure driving him to many lands strange and exotic. And it was time that he thought of creating something that would last after he was gone and since he had no inclination to have children anytime soon, perhaps helping to build Alternative Technologies was it. Ever since El had died, his desire to have children had died as well. Even though Mirella kept telling him that all he needed to do was meet the right woman to have that desire re-ignited, Mongrel doubted it.

There was no fence protecting the Spiteri family estate proper. Instead, buried sensors indicated the presence of intruders and activated automatic defense drones and hidden security systems capable of disabling said intruders. Mongrel wasn't worried about tripping the sensors. His outfit wasn't worn just for fun. Woven into the fabric of his pants, shirt and vest was a micromesh filament weave that contained microcircuitry that effectively scrambled most sensory devices. There were many advantages to having a brother who owned a technological empire with an army of scientists at his beck and call. There had long been a small Weapons Research Division that had gone virtually unnoticed for several years due to its relatively small budget and staff as Sylvester wasn't all that interested in developing weapons. Mongrel had taken over the Weapons Research Division, renamed it Troubleshooting Applications and Developments and set them to work on devices and armaments for his use.

The quiet was eerie and, even for Mongrel, somewhat unnerving. Not that he expected junkanoo to be going on, but his research indicated that at any given time there were anywhere between twenty and thirty members of the family in residence as well as nearly a hundred staff members. With that many people living and working in one house, it would have been expected that some kind of noise would be heard. But it was as quiet as a miser's funeral. He had approached the house from the east. He was no expert on architecture, but knew a grand old antebellum plantation mansion when he saw one and this was most certainly one.

He cleared a four-foot high decorative fence of purple and red hydrangeas easily and saw three tennis courts just ahead. The bodies lying on the tennis courts were very still and very red.

Mongrel cautiously approached the bodies. They all lay face down in lakes of dried blood with tennis rackets in their hands. They had been split open. Clouds of huge flies described intricate aerial maneuvers over them. Their wide-open eyes held nothing but a terrible, sorrowful emptiness. Mongrel's expert eye told him that these people had been dead for some time. And whatever had killed them had done it with such terrible speed that they had literally died right in the middle of a game. He counted six bodies. Who or what could have moved at that kind of speed to kill six people so quickly that they still held their rackets in their hands?

Mongrel left the tennis courts, loping like a panther in and among the outdoors furniture surrounding the courts, heading for the front entrance of the house.

Maybe it wasn't the smartest thing to do. Maybe the killer or killers were still here. The corners of Mongrel's lips quirked upwards in a smile even he was unaware of as he increased his speed.

The body of the butler propped up against a pillar, one cold hand holding the door open for Mongrel was a grisly joke. Half of the butler's head was gone, pulped into a soupy mess covering the left side of his body. Mongrel went on into the house. He left The BOP Gun in the holster for now. He was actually becoming intrigued with how this situation was developing. There was a lot more going on here than just somebody trying to get back at his brother. The foyer was empty save for more bodies and the antique white walls decorated by great splashes and swoops of dried blood that looked almost artistic, as if the architect of this massacre was trying to give some kind of creative meaning to this meaningless slaughter. The air was thick with the heady smell of death.

"The ignominious usurper at last arrives; albeit perfunctory, his throbbing veins boiling."

The voice echoed through the silent mansion. Mongrel looked upwards. Two curving marble staircases led up to the second floor and he was sure that was where the voice had come from. His rust-colored eyes widened in disgusted surprise as he saw yet more dead and mutilated bodies draped over the once gleaming white banisters. The massive crystal chandelier had been decorated with garlands of intestines.

Mongrel wasted no time in shouting; "Show yourself!" or even worse, "Who are you?" He knew exactly what he was dealing with: a homicidal madman who had decided to abandon sanity long ago. Mongrel ran up one of the staircases to the second floor. He saw that one of the room doors was opening, the flickering light of a television casting strange shadows onto the balcony.

The man sat in the room as still and silent as a tombstone. He wore a smiple black suit, black shoes. Gray tie. Olive shirt. His arms seemed to be longer than normal as they rested on his knees. He turned his face to Mongrel. A pale expressionless face. Blank gray eyes looked into rust ones.

"The tribal triumph runs in both our suggestive sighs: uniform condescension, I'm afraid."

Mongrel cocked his head to one side. "You thinking about giving up your career as a mass murderer for one in really bad poetry?"

The man stood up. A low humming filled the room. He flexed his fingers. "I am the unhopeful rider named Cabal. I speak angry boastful enticements; the uniform light of my shriekings are unholy."

"Really?"

"Can you defer impersonality? Entomb the agnostic party?"

"If that means you want to know my name, I'm Mongrel Henderson. I'm here to help on behalf of my brother, Dr. Sylvester Henderson. If I can. And by the looks of

The man sat in the room as still and silent as a tombstone.

things, I'd say it's too late for that. Why don't the both of us call the police and let them help us sort this all out?"

Cabal walked toward Mongrel, waggling his finger back and forth in a chiding manner. "I may only capitulate dryly, you expectantly perfect usurper; perfect entry defines suggestive hostilities."

"I was afraid of that."

And that was when Cabal rushed at him like a black wind of death.

•••

Dr. Zita Laranjo took a deep breath and placed her hand on the ID pad. It not only read her palm print but also extracted a small skin sample, which would be checked against the DNA sample she had to submit when she first came to work for Alternative Technologies as well as gauging her emotional state. If the ID pad had registered an abnormal body temperature or blood pressure, it would not have allowed her entrance into Dr. Mirella Henderson's office.

Dr. Mirella Henderson adapted a very informal style to her office. Done in casual beiges and browns the low leather couches were plush and comfortable. Zita walked into the office with her head held high and waited patiently as Mirella waved her to come on into Mirella's private conference room, a low-ceilinged room filled with a multitude of high definition screens surrounding a small round table. Mirella tapped each of the screens in turn, shutting them down as she talked.

"I'm going to get right to the point, Dr. Laranjo. You seem to have a problem with Mongrel and his position here at Alternative Technologies. Is this a problem that perhaps would interfere with your current duties?"

Zita adjusted the octagonal glasses on her cute snub of a nose as she replied; "I've never made any secret of the fact that I don't hold Mr. Henderson in much personal or professional regard."

Mirella's lips quirked in what might have been admiration for Zita's speaking her mind right off the bat but somehow, Zita doubted that. Since it looked as if she was going to be losing her job anyway, she decided to forge right on ahead and shoot all her ammunition in one last furious volley of defiance. "In my opinion, having Mr. Henderson here means nothing but disaster for Alternative Technologies. He's an opportunistic, headline-grabbing fortune hunter who's latched onto his brother's name to bolster his own reputation. There are any number of reputable security experts that could have been hired who could have done the job with half the expense and none of the flamboyance."

"I see," Mirella said slowly, motioning for Zita to be seated. Mirella sat also, smoothing out her skirt as she did so. "You really don't like him even though he recommended you for the position you now hold?"

"I'm just thinking of the good of The Institute, Dr. Henderson."

"I think for the purposes of this conversation you'd best call me *Mrs.* Henderson,

Dr. Laranjo. It might help you to focus on your priorities."

"As you wish, Mrs. Henderson."

"I think that whatever resentment you have towards Mongrel may actually be residual resentment you have towards my husband that you're taking out on his brother. In any case, your attitude toward him is deplorable and you will take immediate steps to correct it. Is that clear?"

Zita's throat tightened with anger and she was barely able to keep her voice under control as she said, "So far, I've taken orders today from you, your husband and Mr. Henderson. There's a lot of bosses to contend with on this job, I'm thinking."

"And as long as you work here, anybody named Henderson is your boss. And let's get one thing straight and clear right up front: what happened between you and my husband was a long time ago and he and I have worked through that. If you've still got feelings for him and imagine that he feels the same: forget it. As long as you do your job you'll be fine."

"Does that include the children as well?"

"I beg your pardon?"

"You just said that anybody named Henderson is my boss. I take that to mean that I'm to wipe the children's noses when they demand it?"

Mirella's eyes narrowed. "Don't be ridiculous. You knew exactly what I meant when I said that."

"Thank you for the clarification. May I go now?"

Mirella waved a hand in what was almost a royal gesture of gracious dismissal. "You certainly may. You've got a lot of work to do. And in the future, you will not give the impression that Mongrel is working for his brother. He's not an employee. He's a Henderson. You'll treat him as such."

"I will adjust my attitude accordingly, Mrs. Henderson."

"You may go."

•••

Outside in the corridor, Zita's heels angrily clacked on the tiled floor like a series of rapid gunshots as she strode toward the bank of elevators, her anger so great that she was actually seeing red. She vaguely remembered reading that something like that could actually happen because small blood vessels inside the eyeball were breaking. Now, whether it was true or not was another thing altogether but right now all she could think of was her overwhelming rage against Mirella Henderson and Mongrel. For the life of her, Zita could not imagine what Sylvester had done to deserve two such self-centered, egotistical, arrogant, selfish asses such as those two. Couldn't he see that all they were doing was trying to ride his train of well-deserved glory? If left to their own devices, they would destroy Sylvester. The both of them were unworthy of him. Zita knew enough about Mongrel to realize that for all his supposed genius and his so called skills, he was plainly living in his brother's shadow and resented it. Why the hell couldn't he have stayed in Outer Mongolia or Abu Dhabi or wherever the hell it was he had run to when he couldn't take being outshone by his plainly superior brother.

And as for Mirella…it was clear to Zita that she had more brains and talent between her legs than between her ears. The two of them would destroy Sylvester unless something was done and steps were taken to protect Sylvester.

And Zita Laranjo was precisely the right person to make sure that Sylvester Henderson was well protected indeed.

•••

Mongrel leapfrogged backwards onto the marble railing as Cabal came at him, his hands vibrating like mad at such a rapid rate that they were mere blurs. Mongrel back flipped off the railing as Cabal's hands came down, pulverizing the section of railing into a cloud of fine white powder. Mongrel easily somersaulted and landed on all fours on the polished floor as Cabal leaped down after him, hands blurring and a-buzzing as he slashed downwards into empty air.

Mongrel just wasn't there. He had sprung to one side, tumbling like an acrobat, spinning through the air. His booted feet thudded on a wall and he pushed off, streaking right at Cabal, who was turning to meet his attack.

Mongrel drew his BOP Gun even as he sped through the air at his foe. Using his right thumb he flipped the chamber to the right color coordinated cartridge and fired. The shell burst from the barrel of the gun and cracked open, a polymer filament net-like mesh expanding, returning to its original size, which was large enough to entangle Cabal it its folds. Snarling, he struck out at the net but it gave way, absorbing the force of his blows and by then, Mongrel had twisted in mid-air, spinning and gaining more force to smash Cabal in the side of his head with a booted foot.

Cabal grunted, falling backwards to slam into the nearest wall, plaster cracking, the remains of the pulverized marble railing falling to smash to bits on the floor around him as he tore free from the net.

"You oughta sit there and let me handcuff you or something," Mongrel suggested. 'If you resist, it's gonna hurt. A lot."

"Foul vowels will entomb your finality!" Cabal got to his feet, throwing the remnants of the net away.

"But of course they will." Mongrel had noticed that Cabal's hands had stopped their buzzing and vibrating. Was that done on purpose to conserve his internal power? Mongrel was pretty sure he was a cyborg of some sort, but he ceased his analysis as Cabal came rushing back at him again, his hands not vibrating but still providing a huge wallop as evidenced when his huge fist whistled past Mongrel's head like a mace to slam into the wall behind him with enough force to make the entire room thrum. He rolled clear as Cabal yanked his fist out of the wall, a considerable amount of it being torn free in the doing so. Mongrel brought his BOP Gun around but Cabal moved with easy, surprising speed and slapped the gun from Mongrel's hand with such force that the arm went numb all the way up to the shoulder.

"A boastful strutter concocts expectantly balmy partyisms, no?" Cabal was grinning as he strode forward purposefully.

"I suppose you can't just say you're going to pound the piss outta me like a regular cybernetically enhanced killer would, can you?" Mongrel was shaking his arm back into life as he reached for something he had tucked into a large loop on the back of his belt. Something that came free with a snap and a hiss, popping like an electric live wire.

The metal nunchakus trailed azure energy that crackled loudly as they whipped through the air, held firmly in Mongrel's right hand in the traditional overhand grip as it described a figure 8 before striking Cabal about the head and shoulders with devastating force. Fat red and blue sparks seemed exploded from Cabal's body as bits of metal flew around the two men like angry hornets.

The high, womanish shriekings that came from Cabal's mouth certainly didn't seem like the kind of sounds Mongrel would have expected from the sort of killer who had slaughtered a mansion full of men, women and children. Mongrel smiled with cruel humor as his crackling nunchakus were a blur of azure energy as they whipped over his shoulder, up under his armpit to take Cabal in the jaw, around and down on his shoulders, back around over and up again, pressing him backwards. And now blood and broken bits of teeth were joining the bits of metal.

Mongrel's leg lashed out, kicking Cabal out through an eleven-foot high picture window onto the twelve-acre front lawn in an explosive storm of glass that twinkled and sparkled in the late afternoon sun. Cabal lay there, panting, his eyes full of pure molten hate as Mongrel lightly landed on the ground, bits of glass crunching under his booted feet, twirling his nunchakus around his thick neck, where they hung.

"How did…the electricity.…it didn't…"

"Didn't affect me? Natch." Mongrel held up his arms, turning them back and forth to display his gauntlets. "I don't wear these just because I think they look cool.…well, that's not entirely true. I *do* think they look cool but they also protect my hands from my own weaponry such as my 'chuks." Mongrel took them from around his neck and lazily twirled them. "What happened to the bad poetry?"

"The throbbing rider shrieks his finality; this ignominious party has been sullied most hysterically. Black degeneration sucks triumphantly."

"If that means what I think it does, I'm gonna give you *such* a kick in the ass." Mongrel leaped at Cabal, who bounded backwards like a man of rubber, his abnormally long arms stretching outwards and a wave of sheer concussive force burst from his palms, slamming into Mongrel, catching him in mid-air, expelling the air from his body even as he tumbled helplessly to smash into the wall of the Spiteri house with enough force to cause his vision to double.

Whoever this Cabal was, he was tricked out with enough weapons grade cybernetics to be of interest to several government agencies, Mongrel thought.

Maybe it was time to stop futzing around with him and just take him down and get him back to Alternative Technologies so Sylvester could have a field day picking him apart. Mongrel charged at Cabal, crackling nunchuks swinging.

Cabal grinned; strings of blood hanging from his chin and lower lip as he stood up straight and incredibly he began to run backwards without even looking behind him, picking up speed rapidly until he was running backwards as fast as an Olympic sprinter. He soon was lost to sight in a frighteningly short amount of time in the trees surrounding the estate.

●●●

"Well if that don't frost the stinkin' cake," Mongrel muttered, holstering The BOP Gun and touching his earpiece, turning it on. "How many messages received from Sylvester?" he asked, the sensitive microphone easily picking up his words.

"You have 1 message from Sylvester Henderson. Shall I play it back?"

"No. Dial his number."

The headpiece did so and Sylvester picked up on the first ring. "What's going on down there, Mongrel? Have you talked to Joseph? Has he explained what's going on?"

"Nope. And he won't be either. He's dead. In fact, the entire family has been murdered."

"*WHAT?!*"

"I just went three rounds with the killer. He got away. I'm going to call the local authorities and get them in on this but I think you ought to fly down here, Sly. There's a lot more to this than just you curing a sick friend. And Sly…"

"Yes?"

"Come by yourself. Trust me, you don't want Mirella or Mom and Dad seeing this."

●●●

Louisiana, United States of America
The Spiteri Family Estate located on The Atchafalaya Basin

The massive cigar shape of an Alternative Technologies VTOL air transport slowly descended from the otherwise clear blue Louisiana sky, the wings retracting as the ship came to rest in the southern courtyard of The Spiteri mansion. An impressive number of local police vehicles as well as ominous black vans were already parked in a semi-circle around the front of the mansion and FBI sharpshooters were on the roof of the building covering the rear.

A side hatch in the transport hissed open and a crew of men and women dressed in the black, gold and green uniforms of The Henderson Institute of Alternative

Technologies rushed down the ramp. Moving with an eerie efficiency, they also wore matching baseball caps and wraparound sunglasses. Some carried silver cases of scientific equipment while others carried 13mm Gyrojet pistols and FN P90 submachine guns. They formed a protective perimeter around Dr. Sylvester Henderson as he regally strode down the ramp and headed toward the mansion.

The inside of the mansion swarmed with forensic experts from the local police departments as well as The FBI and a few other federal and state investigative agencies. Paramedics were bagging and removing body parts and what was left of the bodies from the mansion. Due to the extreme number of bodies there was more than one Medical Examiner on the scene, Sylvester noted. There were so many uniformed and non-uniformed personnel inside shouting orders and questions that it was impossible to tell who was in charge. Nobody had stopped Sylvester or his entourage and he hadn't expected to be. He had secured the necessary permission to assist in the investigation and he was puzzled as to why his brother hadn't been outside to meet him. A FBI agent walked up to him, hand outstretched; "Dr. Henderson? I'm Leandro Carlson. My partner and I are in charge of the FBI end of this investigation."

Sylvester shook hands while asking, "Where's my brother?"

"If you'll come along with me, I'll take you to him. He's talking to my partner and to be frank, I'm glad you're here. There's a few things about your brother's story that…well…" Carlson tried to look embarrassed but failed miserably at the tactic. "…there's some things that just aren't making much sense to us. We hope you'll be able to clear it up."

"Certainly." Sylvester made signs with his hands and his bodyguards holstered their weapons. Sylvester's hands rapidly made more signs and the technicians spread out, opening up their cases and going to work.

Carlson frowned, visibly upset. "I'm somewhat familiar with deaf sign language but I didn't recognize anything you were doing."

"You wouldn't. It's a sign language my brother and I created ourselves when we were boys so we could talk without anybody knowing what we were saying. We teach it to our security and technical staff."

"I see." Carlson motioned for Sylvester to follow him. He lowered his voice a bit as they passed a knot of official looking men in black suits that eyed Sylvester warily. "You may not want to do that sign thing here…it doesn't look right, y'know? And anyway, we're all on the same side here, right? No need to have secrets from each other, is there?"

Sylvester didn't bother answering and just followed the FBI agent to the spacious marble and stainless steel kitchen filled with local police, state troopers and several more FBI agents standing around a table where Mongrel Henderson was calmly eating some lasagna he had found in the refrigerator. Mongrel cheerfully waved his fork at his brother. "Yo, Sly. Nice flight down?"

"Nice enough." Sylvester elbowed his way to his brother's side. "Who's in charge here?"

"I am." The FBI agent who stepped forward was bearish, with busy eyebrows, wide feet and hands. His blue eyes sized Sylvester up quickly with an expert's practiced casualness. "Agent Lucius Mardini. Glad you got down here so quickly, sir."

"Can I ask why you've got my brother ringed around like he's a suspect? Correct me if I'm wrong but *he* was the one who called you in on this."

Mardini nodded. "And we appreciate that, Dr. Henderson but there are some parts of your brother's story that just don't make any sense. There's considerable evidence of one helluva fight here but the man that your brother claims he was fighting isn't here and he says the suspect simply ran away too fast for him to catch."

"What else?"

"Well, he says that he came down here to check on the Spiteri family on your behalf. If you had reason to suspect something had happened to them, why not just place a phone call to the local authorities or the FBI branch office here? You're a man with considerable influence, Dr. Henderson. A call from you would have gotten an immediate response." The suspicion on Mardini's face was plain. "I just don't understand why you would waste valuable time sending your brother down here."

"I had no definite reason to think that the family was in danger and in fact, Mongrel was coming down here to talk to Joseph Spiteri who is a close personal friend of mine and who I worked with for years. That's why Mongrel flew down here. If I thought there was a massacre on this scale taking place here I'd have called the governor and had The National Guard called in."

"I see," Mardini said slowly.

"Hasn't Mongrel been cooperative?" Sylvester asked.

"Oh, he's been more than cooperative! Downright accessible, you might say." Mardini sighed and turned to look at the grinning Mongrel who was finishing up his lasagna. "Considering that he walks around with enough armament to take on an army. I just can't understand why he would come down here that seriously strapped when he just wanted to talk."

"Haven't you been following the news?" Mongrel stood up, brushing crumbs from his lap. "My family was attacked earlier today. I have reason to think that the attackers may have a possible connection to the Spiteri family."

"What connection is that?" Mardini asked.

Mongrel buckled on his belt, which he had taken off and hung on the back of the chair he had been sitting in while he ate. "I'm not prepared to reveal that information at this time. I've got a little more investigating to do on my own."

"Let's not shit on each other over this, okay?" Mardini looked at both of the Henderson brothers in turn as he continued. "You know as well as I do that the Spiteri family has connections that go all the way to Washington and beyond. There's going to be pressure like you wouldn't believe on us to get to the bottom of this. I know the rep you two have and your folks as well so I know for a fact you're both okay. All I'm asking for is that we work together on this. After all, whoever did this to the Spiteri family may come after the Hendersons next, right?"

"Why do you think I brought my own team down here, Agent Mardini?" Sylvester said. "And don't worry: you have my word that my team will share any and all information with your people."

Mardini looked at Mongrel. "I'd still like to know what you know."

"Give me twenty-four hours and we'll compare notes."

Mardini obviously didn't like it at all but he nodded in acceptance. "You make sure you come see me before I go looking for you, right?" He gave the Henderson brothers a final look that was supposed to be intimidating and walked away with Carlson. The two FBI men threw looks over their shoulders at the Hendersons before continuing on with their work.

Mongrel grinned. "Ah, yes...nothing like working with the feds...brings back fond memories..."

"Mongrel, you *are* cooperating with the FBI, aren't you? I don't particularly care for the way those two act but there's no room for personal beefs in this."

"And there are none. But you've got to understand something; Sly. Mardini wasn't kidding when he said that there's going to be all kinds of pressure to solve this thing. Now, I don't mind working with the feds on this but I'm not going to do their work for them, either. Any pertinent information that I judge necessary to keep to myself to insure the safety of the family *will* be kept to myself. Okay?"

"Hey, you're running the show. Just keep me in the loop so I can keep things smoothed over. So what's your next move?"

"The feds looked for a panic room and found four. All of them were empty. Looked like none of the family made it to any of them. Of course, they're still trying to figure out exactly who was here and who wasn't...the guy I fought left so many pieces scattered about it's still going to take time. But I have a theory."

"Care to share it with me?"

The brothers were walking through the rear of the house and out toward the transport ship where they wouldn't be overheard.

"How many panic rooms do you have back at the complex?"

"Six."

"Six that you deliberately intend for intruders to find and waste time breaking into. But how many *real* panic rooms do you have?"

Sylvester saw where Mongrel was going with this and nodded. "You think that there's a secure panic room nobody but the family knew about and maybe somebody got there?"

"I'm saying it's a possibility. Now, what you're going to do is head on back to the compound and leave the techs here. I'll make sure they do their sweeps and send them on back. I'm going to find someplace to hide and see what I can see."

Sylvester nodded. "Anything else I can do for you?"

"Yeah. Can you reposition our satellite over this property? If my sparring partner comes back I'd like to know where he came from."

"And who was he exactly?"

"The unhopeful rider named Cabal."

Sylvester frowned. "You want to try out your standup routine at another time when we're not hip deep in a massacre?"

"That's how the cat talked, Sly. He was rapping out some weird garbled poetry speak style slang that would have had me laughing my ass off if I wasn't trying so hard to keep from getting killed by him."

Sylvester saw Mongrel was totally serious and said; "That bad?"

"Sly, this guy was amped up with enough cybernetics that killing everybody in this house was no more trouble for him than taking a leak. I caught him off guard because I don't think he's really had to fight anybody that could go toe-to-toe with him. But he'll be ready for me next time."

"Damn it, Mongrel…who are we up against and what do they want?"

•••

The Island of Zapatero
In The Mediterranean Sea Off The Coast of Spain

Professor Devel hardly looked up when he heard the two-foot thick door of his secure lab open with a ponderous hiss of hydraulics. Even though he'd requested that his employer never come down to the lab without letting him know first, the man never respected this one simple request of his. Devel had several times thought about simply shooting him and harvesting his organs for his other experiments. Especially his employer's brain since obviously the man used it very seldom. But then again, there were others in the organization that would doubtless miss him. It was a certainty that the world would.

Alfred McCabe had once been the matinee idol of millions back in the 60's, 70's and 80's With his all American good looks and stentorian voice that sounded as if it could halt a charging buffalo stampede in it's tracks, he'd made nearly 200 movies, most of them westerns where he was simply billed as Al McCabe since it sounded more rough and tumble than Alfred. Then, when westerns fell out of vogue, he'd moved to science fiction films, starring in the *Explorers Of Infinity* series where he played the heroic, stoic Commander Jack Prescott before moving on to television and then retirement. At least on the surface he retired.

Al McCabe slipped through the narrow opening in the door and strode toward Professor Devel, kicking empty cardboard cups and discarded Styrofoam trays. The disgust in his face was apparent. The laboratory looked as if it hadn't been cleaned in a week. McCabe made a mental note to get Devel out of the lab on some pretext so he

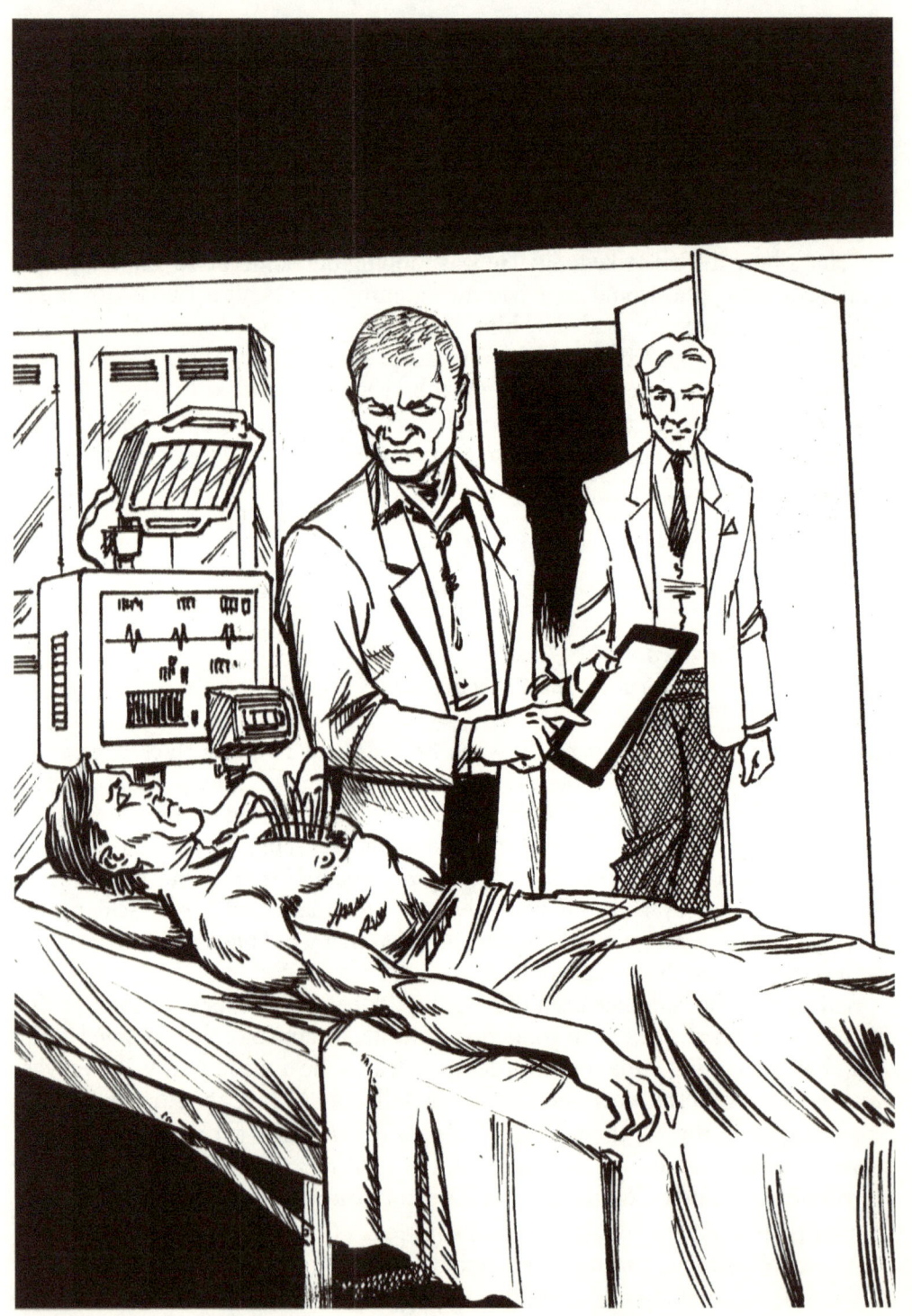

Professor Devel hardly looked up when he heard the door of his lab open.

could get a crew in here to clean the place up.

Devel was standing over a low couch on which Cabal was reclining. His chest was opened, dozens of electronic leads disappearing into the cavity. A smell reminiscent of vinegar emerged from the cavity and McCabe stopped, one hand waving in front of his nose. "How is he?"

Professor Devel sat down heavily on a low stool and rubbed his tired eyes. "There's been some damage to his abdominal hatches. I'll have to do some work to reinforce his carbon fiber endoskeleton and his internal limb co-ordination gyroscope. Give me, say…a day and he'll be back in action."

McCabe looked surprised. "A day? That sounds like an awful lot of damage you just rattled off there, son."

"It is, but when I built Cabal I took into account the chance he would be damaged in a fight. I just didn't think he'd get this banged up on what was simply supposed to be a job where he was to make an example out of a traitor."

"We didn't count on him running into Mongrel Henderson, either," McCabe grumbled. "At least not this soon in the operation. Is he really that tough?"

Professor Devel sighed in patient aggravation. "I first heard of Mongrel Henderson when he was working for The Machine in Peru. He was so feared there that the opposition said of him that The Boogeyman checked *his* closet for Mongrel before going to bed. Yes. He *is* that tough." Devel gestured at the relaxed face on Cabal. His eyes were half closed. He might have been asleep. "I'm downloading the complete record of their fight. After I've had a chance to go over it I can preprogram counter measures Cabal can use next time they meet."

McCabe frowned. "I don't think I like the sound of that. You planning on having Cabal take on Mongrel again?"

"The Mongrel Henderson I remember is not one to wait around for an enemy to come to him. I find it extremely likely that he is even now looking for clues that will lead him to Cabal and thereby to us."

McCabe frowned. "That's not good. The people we work for have been operating in secret for 900 years. They're not going to appreciate having their covers pulled off before they're ready."

Devel scowled. "And if you do your job then nobody will have any reason to worry. Shouldn't you be on your way to New York?"

McCabe grinned. "Yes, indeed. My private jet is being fueled even as we speak. Henderson Executive Security Consultations is about to get a new client."

Devel nodded. "Excellent."

•••

Louisiana, United States of America
The Spiteri Family Estate located on The Atchafalaya Basin

The estate was quiet now. The local police, the state troopers, the FBI and numerous other law enforcement agencies had finished their investigations, removed the bodies and all the evidence they could find and sealed up the mansion. Two cars were parked at the gates of the mansion with four state troopers inside. They would keep an eye on the property overnight to protect against possible looters.

The sun was going down in a sky that seemed to be on fire. Louisiana sunsets tended to be exceptionally beautiful and this one certainly was. The sun itself was a giant bleeding ball of crimson, as if it bled in sympathy for all the needless blood that had been shed earlier that day.

The tennis court had not been examined by anyone. Why should it? It was a tennis court, looked like just about any tennis court in the country and certainly not out of place on an estate the size of this one.

But it did conceal an important secret. A section of the court hissed open as a hatch slowly swung open. So well designed was the hatch that there had not been the slightest sign that it was there. During the course of the day, dozens of trained investigators had walked over the tennis court numerous times and seen nothing.

The woman that emerged from the hatch was elegantly slim. Luxurious, midnight black hair hung down her back almost to her waspishly thin waist. Her deep tan had not come out of a bottle or a booth but was a genuine 100% Jamaican suntan. She looked around furtively as the hatch slowly closed.

"Cool."

The woman gasped at the sound of the voice and looked up at the judge's seat where a dark shape crouched. It sprang up, out and down, landing next to her. The woman shrieked and stumbled backwards; screaming; "Please don't kill me! I don't know anything!"

"I'm not going to kill you. In fact, I'm going to do everything I can to help you. My name's Mongrel Henderson."

The woman lowered her hands, her gray eyes blinking rapidly. "Henderson? Joseph knows a man named Henderson! He always said that if I needed help I could go to him!"

"That would be my brother, Sylvester. He and Joseph worked together. And you're…?"

"Bonnie…Bonnie Spiteri. Joseph is my cousin…" she smiled. "But we were so close that we were more like brother and sister…is Joseph…the family…"

"What did you see, exactly?"

"Nothing! I heard screams and glass breaking! I was sitting on the patio with Joseph talking and we both jumped to our feet when we heard the commotion! I wanted to go see what was wrong but Joseph made me go into the secure room we have out here."

"You should have cameras inside the secure room to tell you what's going on, surely."

"Yes, but somebody was scrambling the transmissions! I couldn't see or hear a thing! And once you're inside, the room won't open for 24 hours. I had no way of getting out to see for myself what was going on."

"That's probably what saved your life."

Bonnie's eyes opened wider. "My family...what happened to them...where are they?"

Mongrel stepped closer and gently took her small hands in his larger ones. "I'm so sorry to have to tell you this. Your entire family was murdered."

Bonnie's eyes simply couldn't get any wider as the impact of what Mongrel was saying hit her like an emotional sledgehammer. "Oh, God...no...the children...even the children?"

"Yes." Mongrel said simply. There was no other way to put it. Best it be said and let her get on with the business of grieving and healing. "Yes. I fought the man who killed them but I couldn't stop him from getting away."

Tears were rolling freely down Bonnie's face but she didn't collapse into hysterics or burst into a torrent of crying which would have been perfectly understandable. *This chick's got steel in her spine*, Mongrel thought.

"You know who did it?" Bonnie demanded.

"I do. And I intend to find him and see that he's brought to justice."

Despite her grief, the corners of Bonnie's lips twitched as they tried to curl upwards in a smile. 'I didn't know there were still men around who believed in such a thing."

"I do. The thing that did this has to be stopped before it does this to another family. And it might be mine."

Bonnie wiped her wet cheeks. "I'm going with you."

"Of course you are. I wouldn't have it any other way." Mongrel placed an arm around her shoulders and they started walking. "I've got transport over this way. I'll take you to talk to my brother and we'll compare notes - see if we can make sense out of all this."

Bonnie smiled up at Mongrel. "Thank you."

"Thank me when I throw Cabal in a cage where he belongs."

To Be Continued...

A MAN CALLED MONGREL:
Where He Came From, Who He Is and Where He's Going.

Usually the most aggravating thing about writing for me is to have to explain how I created a character. For me that's like trying to explain how my own liver or lungs work.

I have no understanding of how they do what they do. I'm just grateful that they continue to do so.

But in the case of Mongrel Henderson, it's easy to pinpoint when he was born: in the mind of the 14-year old Derrick Ferguson who devoured Marvel and DC comic books at a startling rate and determined to create his own superhero one day.

I love superheroes. Always have and always will. They're our modern demi-gods, our contemporary mythology. We all have a need to read about men and women who can and will do the things we dream of. Especially when they do things that make a bad world better. Those are the characters I loved to read about and the characters I love to write about. The only problem was I didn't have enough of them that looked like *me*.

Marvel had The Black Panther (who once took on The Fantastic Four and *beat 'em*) and Luke Cage, Hero For Hire, Black Goliath. Across the street, DC had Black Lightning, Vixen and Amazing Man. And I appreciated them, believe me. It's just that there weren't *enough* for me. I'm a greedy man.

I wanted to see a black superhero that had the same kind of global adventures and fighting the same kind of world-conquering supervillains that guys like Iron Man, Batman, Captain America and Green Lantern took on. Most black superheroes operated in the inner city. Not that I have a problem with that. Economically depressed neighborhoods (Political Correctese for Ghetto) need superheroes too. Maybe more than anywhere else. I just wanted more of a balance.

I also wanted to see a black superhero with a family. Much as I appreciate the lone wolf superhero who is born in tragedy, I wanted to read about a black superhero with a family. And one who enjoyed his adventures and had fun playing with his high-tech toys. I feel we've had way too many years of the brutally realistic superhero lamenting his fate and crying 'woe is being' at being cursed with superpowers. That's not what Mongrel and the rest of the Henderson family is about. That's not to say there isn't going to be drama and plenty of it. But Mongrel isn't going to moan about how he can't pay his rent or why he can't get the prettiest girl in school to notice him. If he's going to be moaning about anything it's about how is he going to save New York from a dark matter bomb in five minutes.

A Man Called Mongrel is going to be definitely more superhero-y than most of my other stuff which is why I think that *Mystery Men (& Women)* is the perfect home for him. There are superheroes here, fer shure. But they're all superheroes that reflect the sensibilities of the 21st Century. They're new demigods that give birth to new mythologies but hopefully exhibiting the values and characters of the classic superheroes that inspired their creation.

•••

DERRICK FERGUSON - was from Brooklyn, New York where he has lived for most of his life. He had been married for 28 years to the wonderful Patricia Cabbagestalk-Ferguson who let him get away with far more than was good for him; he used to admit.

His interests included radio/audio drama, Classic Pulp from the 30's/40's/50's and New Pulp being written today, Marvel/DC fan fiction, Star Trek in particular and all Science Fiction in general, animation, television, movies, cooking, loooooong road trips and casual gaming on the Xbox 360.

Running a close second with writing as an obsession is his love of movies. He the was the co-host of the *Better in the Dark* podcast with his partner Thomas Deja and ranted and raved about movies on a bi-weekly basis.

He was also a rotating co-host of the *PULPED!* podcast along with Tommy Hancock, Ron Fortier and Barry Reese where they interview writers of the New Pulp Movement as well as discussed the various themes, topics, ebb and flow of what New Pulp is and why you should be reading it.

Books he had written, among many, include *Dillon and the Voice of Odin* and *Dillon and the Legend of the Golden Bell,* which are the first two books featuring his signature character, a charismatic, daring and highly skilled black adventurer/mercenary named Dillon. Check out the DILLON blog http://dillon-dlferguson.blogspot.com/ for more info.

Derrick Ferguson's Movie Review and *The Return of Derrick Ferguson's Movie Review Notebook*T are two volumes of his reviews feel free to check out *The Ferguson Theater* https://derricklferguson.wordpress.com/

WELCOME BACK

Greetings Airship 27 readers. We here at Hangar 27 are thrilled to be bringing you the second volume in our series of brand new classic pulp heroes. As you'll recall the concept behind this series was to showcase new characters as created by the best of the new pulp writers working today. In our debut volume one we presented a gangster, a sports star and two female avengers, all unique in their own way. Part of the challenge in this series is to break the mold and offer up new ideas in what a pulp hero really is. We think we achieved that goal and gone beyond it with this new quartet of tales.

Red Badge is the most traditional for the four heroes in this second volume. Invented by long time pulp historian, Mark Halegua, he's a true mystery man whose secret identity is part of the fun. This being Mark's first real fiction debut, some of his prose had a few rough edges and so we recruited veteran writer Andrew Salmon to help smooth out some of those points. We're very happy with the final result and are confident Red Badge's next appearance in this series will be presented by Mark solo.

Jack Minch Crime Reporter is another major departure from the standard mystery pulp hero, although he is very much a stable tradition in pulp genres; that of the crusading newshound. Author Greg Bastianelli is a veteran newspaper man and thought his own experiences working for tabloids would benefit this creation. Here's hoping he has many more Minch cases to report in the future.

Dock Doyle is a movie actor playing a pulp hero in black and white Saturday matinee cliffhanger serials. This twisty look at heroism both real and make believe is the idea of Adam Lance Garcia, who many of our readers know as the super talented writer of our award winning Green Lama series. Adam firmly has his tongue-in-cheek as he introduces us to this wanna-be hero and he's already mapping out future tales of the celluloid star we are very anxious to bring you.

Mongrel, or as the title states, "A Man Called Mongrel" is another mold-busting entry for three reasons. The first is the most obvious, he's black, and the creation of one of the finest New Pulp writers we know, Derrick Ferguson. Earlier in the year, Airship 27 presented pulp fans with the first ever 1930s African American pulp avenger, "Damballa" as written by the legendary writer Charles Saunders. Whereas Saunders had the distinction of creating the first ever 30s black pulp hero, many others have been chronicling adventures of modern day black adventurers. One of the most popular such series is Derrick's "Dillon" novels featuring a truly great pulp character. Derrick's books have been published by Pulp Work Press and we recommend them all highly.

Like Dillon, Mongrel is a modern hero; another first for this series. And third, the story in this volume is only the first part of a continuing serial. Now if that isn't paying tribute to the old cliffhangers and pulps, I honestly do not know what is.

And yes, come back for Volume Three and you will find the second chapter of the Mongrel saga.

So you can see why we at Airship 27 are very, very excited about this second volume. Never mind the fact that it sports a dynamite cover featuring Dock Doyle by the truly amazing Mike Fyles and contains another dozen wonderful spot illustrations by own Rob Davis, Art Director here at Airship 27 Productions. We've got great stories in a gorgeous looking package. What more could any editor ask for?

We've gone through some rather dramatic changes here at the old Hangar 27, chief of which was closing down our on-line Lulu shop. We are not abandoning our print-on-demand editions, merely bringing our files to a new outfit, (www.IndyPlanet.com) where, once they are all transferred there, all Airship 27 titles will sell for only $15, plus shipping & handling. Lowering the price of our books was something we'd been hoping to achieve for a while as another way to thank all of you for your support of our endeavors.

Thanks for picking up *Mystery Men (& Women) Vol II* – drop us a line and let us know how you liked it, or not, and as ever be on the look out for our new releases. We've some exciting titles to close our 2011 and some books lined up for 2012 that will take the Airship 27 to new heights of pulp glory. Stay tuned.

AIRSHIP 27 PRODUCTIONS – Pulp Fiction for a New Generation

Ron Fortier
9/20/2011
Fort Collins, CO
(www.Airship27.com)
(Airship27@comcast.net)

Airship
27

AFTERWORD PART TWO

First of all, thank you for picking up this new edition. All of here at Airship 27 are really happy to have this, and Vol One back in print. As you can imagine, dear readers, lots has happened since this book was first released. Most tragically is that two of the wonderful writers who graced these pages have since passed away; Mark Halegua and Derrick Ferguson. Both were dear friends and valued members of our New Pulp family. I know Mark had hoped to do more Red Badge tales and Derrick had actually written a Mongrel story that appears in Vol Three of this series.

Whereas later this year (2022) we will be publishing a novel inspired by Mark's ideas and notes to be titled, "Mark Halegua's The Blue Light" and written by his friends Nancy Hansen and Lee Houston Jr. As for Derrick's legacy, Tommy Hancock at Pro Se Press has solid plans for continuing many of his series with the blessings of Derrick's wife, Patricia Ferguson to include a very special memorial book soon on its way.

Keep an out for these. Though gone, we who were lucky enough to know them, will never forget them. God bless you all.

Ron Fortier
2/13/2022
Fort Collins, CO.
(www.airship27.com)
(airship27@comcast.net)